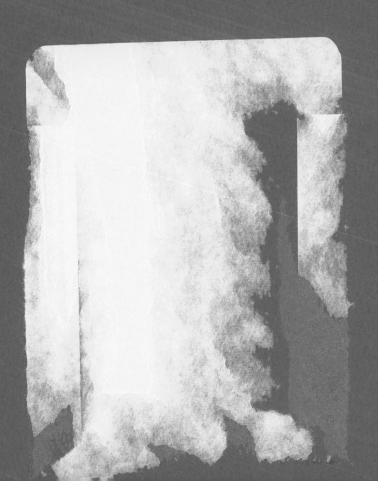

The Life and Death of
YELLOW BIRD

by James Forman

The
Life and Death
of
YELLOW BIRD

James Forman

FARRAR, STRAUS AND GIROUX
New York

FOR SANDRA BONDY,
*with her generous heart
and ready laughter*

Contents

I

The Corpse in the Greasy Grass

The thunder beings had danced all that night in the northwest, beating their terrible drums, throwing spears of fire, and Yellow Bird, tossing in restless sleep, had heard them. Born in a cloud, the thunder beings had ridden black horses with flaming manes. "Your grandfathers are calling you," they had told him in voices like singing. They had pulled him up and carried him away to where the rainbow arched over them with many-colored flames, and he had seen a vision of another world through the lightning flashes, a land lovely beyond song. He saw all this for one breathless instant, a vision on the bright sky, but more intense than dreaming, more real than life under a summer sun. Then it was gone. He struggled to retain what he had glimpsed, but he was left with nothing but a vanishing sense of loveliness, overlaid with a tremulous sense of morning. Sweet as dew, pure as mountain water, the new awareness filled him.

His awakening eyes first focused on the tepee pole, a stripe of turquoise under the gleaming sun. It would shine on great doings this day. "Dead white men, they fall into our camp!" Sitting Bull had proclaimed, and the time was near. Yellow Bird had heard him. "The time for thunder in our mouths is past," Sitting Bull had said. "We must have lightning in our hands." Beside the Sacred Deer Medicine Rocks the great chief had announced this to all the gathered tribes, especially to the braves ringed round by war to the death such as they had never been before. The white man, the Wasichu, was sending his bluecoat soldiers against them. Scouts had brought back the word. Three Stars Crook moved his walk-alongs from the south. Gibbon, the One Who Limps, marched from the setting of the sun, and Long Hair Custer, the Killer of Squaws, rode with his horse soldiers from the land of the dawning. So, for this great battle to come, Yellow Bird had watched the braves fell the sun-dance tree with stone axes in the old way. No white man's metal must touch this holy thing. Many ponies and gaily shouting warriors had dragged it to the sun circle. Then all had come to see its branches hung with banners and with the images of men and buffalo. It held the promise of great strength, and mothers brought their newborn babies so that its power and courage would sink into them.

Yellow Bird lay in the tepee, remembering how the old men, sitting quietly in the great circle, had waited for the dance to begin. Their eagle-wing fans had moved slowly in their hands, spreading the fragrant smoke of red willow bark from their pipes upon the sun-filled air. All here were holy, the two-leggeds and the four-leggeds; all were children of the great mystery. Even before the first tap-tapping of the drums, before the first feet stirred the dust, Yellow Bird had felt the power drawing him as surely as the sun draws water.

Those who would dance had been painted, legs and forearms white, bodies black, faces covered with a large blue sun as it appeared to eyes that had gazed on it too long. Some had already stared at that flaming wonder until they were nearly blind, but the more serious ones had given themselves to blood and pain. Yellow Bird had watched in horrid fascination as iron skewers, big around as the shaft of an arrow, were driven into the chest muscles of Billy Fine Weather, under and out again, with the blood washing down. Then the skewers had been attached to long rawhide thongs hung from the top of the sun-dance pole. Away they had danced, those painted bloody braves, whirling, stamping, up on tiptoe, jerking against the pain until they fell unconscious or the skewers broke free. There had been many performing in this great year of war, wearing a red path in the dust.

Yellow Bird was still too young to participate, but outside the circle of the tireless dancers he had found his feet moving to the drums. His eyes had sought out the sun until, like a mouth full of fire, white, blue, green, overflowing, it had drawn him down. In a blinding instant he had seen a place bright as the sky, a land of rich green rolling hills and browsing game. As he saw he danced, and as he danced he wondered. Where was this place? And what of the voice that spoke from the glare, telling him to go there? In dreams he had heard that voice before, as he had heard the thunder people in the night, and he had spoken of it to his mother as he would speak of a conversation with a friend. But this was in scorching daylight. It was something no child dare tell of, for surely it was meant for one greater than he.

How long that vision lasted Yellow Bird would never know. He knew only that when his sight and hearing had returned he was stretched in the shade of the sun-dance house. The drummers had been tapping softly then, for the great one, Sitting Bull, had shoved into the circle of dancers. He had danced clumsily because of an old wound from a Crow bullet in his foot. Big-bodied, big-nosed, strong of jaw and narrow of lip, Sitting Bull had the curiously soft and dainty hands of a maiden, though those who knew him said that beneath the flesh were the sinews of a wolf. Now his dancing was done, his ordeal was about to begin. Sitting Bull had performed the ritual many times before, and his back and breast were welted with memorials to pain. This time it had been the cutting away of flesh from his arms, fifty small strips from each. Without a change of expression, without a flinch or the blinking of an eye, he had sat there as the hammer and chisel had done their tedious work. Then, like a red tower, he had stood alone. To Yellow Bird he had looked as big as a god against the sun. For a long time Sitting Bull had remained there, attentive not to the drums or the dancers but to something further away that only he could hear. At last he had taken a wavering step forward and back, and he had thrust up his hands as though the sun were a weight upon him. Then the vision had come from his lips, no private thing but a calling forth in a great voice: "In the sky I see soldiers!" Yellow Bird had looked up, seen only the sun pierced blue. "Like grasshoppers they fall dead into our camp!"

Several days had now passed since Sitting Bull had seen the future, and the great encampment on the Greasy Grass had grown. The talk was of scalps and blood, and there was much war dancing around the fires at night. This was the season of the warrior, the Moon of Making Fat, when the grass stood fresh and high. In the mornings the braves slept late, saving themselves for battle, and when Yellow Bird arose the camp was still. He was alone in the tepee. There was no old woman hunched up in the shadows like a half-blind owl to tell him what to do. No shield hung outside, sacred from the touch of strangers. He was born of no Indian marriage. Some called him the No Father with something that was derisive

[6]

and something that was sad. When he'd been very small, his mother had simply called him Pot Belly, and later, Slow, but now that his hair was down to his shoulders, only one name would do: Yellow Bird. His hair was the color of prairie grass and it set him apart. He and his mother belonged to the People, and yet there was an awareness only just growing in him that they did not belong, could never belong, no matter what he did. This was not for want of trying, and when he emerged from the tepee he did so in the proper manner, though no one was there to reprimand him. He trod the long circle just as the seasons and the sun and the moon made their rounds.

In these hot days the cooking fire was kept outside, and just now it was unattended. All around arched the great sacred hoop of tepees, tepees beyond counting. They crowded to the banks of the Greasy Grass, for many tribes were there, each in its sacred circle—Sans Arc, Hunkpapa, Oglala, Miniconjou, Blackfeet, Santee, Brûlé—and even crippled old Black Elk had come in from the Red Cloud reservation with a few lodges. With him was Red Cloud's son, carrying a silver-mounted rifle that had been presented to his father by the Wasichu chief in Washington.

Sometimes in this Moon of Making Fat the cold wind blew from the mountains, bringing the glittering hailstones big as prairie chicken eggs, but this year was hot and full of dust born on a south wind. Yellow Bird, glancing at the young sky already fusing with heat that prickled the hairs on the back of his arm, knew that the hottest day in a hot season was at hand. Already the sky singers swooped low over the distant river, saluting the sun with their outstretched wings. Beyond, where the hills stood tall and black against the sky, eagles would be rising on the heat currents. The mountain lion would have returned to his lair, tongue lolling, and the young antelope left by its mother in a patch of bull-tongue cactus would quiver, not with dawn cold, but with fear of the prowling coyote.

Yellow Bird ate quickly from the pot that his mother had left on the coals. She must have gone for water or to dig turnips with the other women. She had trusted him to keep the fire. The food that he ate was a source of pride as well as strength, for the jack rabbit had been brought down by his own bow. He would try his arm against antelope before the cherries ripened. Let them fear him in their brushy dens; he knew where they hid.

As Yellow Bird ate, he observed the crier proceeding around the tepee circle. It was so large he did not walk, but rode, a pack of mucus-yellow dogs at his heels. His voice was a drone at first, the words lost, but as he approached, Yellow Bird heard him tell of the hunters returning, sounding the wolf howl of danger. There were bluecoats still in the valley of the Rosebud, where they had been beaten. There were more bluecoats nearing the Greasy Grass. How many? It scarcely seemed to matter. If fifty Modoc warriors could hold off fifty times their number of white men, then the People who had gathered here at the Greasy Grass could turn back the bluecoats even if they fell upon the camp as thick as locusts.

There was talk among the elders that the old days had returned, the good days of dancing, courting, and hunting. Others said, "If the old days are back again, where are the buffalo?" The buffalo chips were thin on the prairies and the trees were no longer rubbed smooth by the backs of the shedding herds. But if these were not quite the old days, which

Yellow Bird knew of only from stories, they were like nothing he had ever experienced before. He could hardly believe there were so many warriors, most of them lazing about, having kill talks, or flirting with the girls. The warriors still wore their braids behind, like children, and this was fitting and proper since they might die at any time in battle. It was up to the others to work, the boys to guard the herds of ponies, which had already cropped the grass for miles around, and to hunt the antelope and the few buffalo that grazed in the valley of the Big Horn. It was up to the women to keep the camp, and to the old Big Bellies to make wise decisions for them all.

So Yellow Bird's camp circle waited for the coming of the bluecoats on that never-to-be-forgotten morning. They, the Tsistsista, or the People, as they called themselves, the Cheyenne in the white man's tongue, had marched first into the Greasy Grass and had the place of honor at the western head of the other camp circles. Only the narrower, longer smoke flap of their tepees distinguished the camp of the Cheyenne from the different circles of the Sioux tribe. To the southeast, along the sluggish banks of the Greasy Grass, was the circle of the Oglala. Next to them were the Brûlé, then the Sans Arc, Miniconjou, the Blackfeet Sioux, and farthest south and close to the river, the Hunkpapa. There Sitting Bull, who had brought them all together, had his camp. There were other great war leaders among them: Two Kettles and No Bows, Gall and Black Moon, Two Moons and Old Bear; but greatest of them all was the war chief of the Oglala, Crazy Horse.

When he had finished eating, Yellow Bird thanked the rabbit for giving him its strength and fleetness of foot so that its spirit would not discredit him with its fellows and make them harder to catch. Then he took his Osage bow strung with twisted deer sinew and ashen arrows trued with wild turkey feathers, which were the sign of his people. The tips were forged from fire-hardened hoop iron, and with luck he could bring down another jack rabbit if they were not all hunted out toward the river. He was not the only boy with such ideas. Many were drawn over the meadow toward the river. Yellow Bird saw the grass bend down, then spring up again as they passed, running, shouting, scalping the prairie flowers with wooden hatchets, winning the battle of the Rosebud all over again.

All their play had to do with that fight. As long as the People sang songs, that day would belong to Crazy Horse. He had been chosen war leader over all the Sioux and over Yellow Bird's people as well, for Crazy Horse's wife came from a Cheyenne lodge and that made the two tribes close. "Now we are one People," Crazy Horse had said. "All one tribe as in the old times. When they went out in those days, they went as one man, and if one did not wish to fight he went away and no one called after him." What Crazy Horse had said was simple. He was a simple man, not large or powerful, but he had a fury that shook and trembled in his voice, not as a leaf trembles on the wind but as the vibrations of a drum. He was the spark that set a trail of gunpowder burning in all who heard him. He offered them no visions of victory as Sitting Bull had done. He spoke of war, and how it must be won.

There was the Indian way, he had said, which was a kind of game: a game for glory, for counting coup, for taking horses. That was the proper way to fight the Crow or the Shoshoni. But against the bluecoat soldiers of the white man they must fight differently. They must think, as the Wasichu did, only of killing. In battle, Indians thought of scalps taken, friends wounded or slain, but white men thought of lines of battle and massing their fire. They had no wives to worry about, no sons to protect, only pay-women sometimes. "The Wasichu live to kill, and each man does what he is told. We must remember to hear our leader and charge together. No one must stop for horses or scalps until the fight is over. Now let every warrior, if he agrees, call out with a great shout."

A clamor of voices had arisen, and the din of bows beaten against arrows. As he had stood above them on the rocks, the cliffs golden behind him, the sun burning in his feathers, Crazy Horse had seemed as much of the race of Gods as had Sitting Bull. With such great leaders, Yellow Bird had no fear that they might lose.

Only after they had danced to the war drum, a pulse quicker than the excited heart, had the braves moved out in the old, old way—pipe bearers, scouts ahead, dog soldiers on the flanks to keep back the wild young warriors who might try to ride ahead for glory's sake and spoil the plan. Yellow Bird had shouted. Around him, eagle-bone whistles had screamed the warriors on their way into that bad country of ravines toward the Rosebud Valley. A day of waiting, and a night, and then the first tales had come back from the Rosebud of Crazy Horse leading his braves with a stripped and violent fury that had kept them together as he had planned. Always Crazy Horse had taken the lead, leaping from his pony to fire so that each shot would find a target, and so they had driven the dust-reddened soldiers back upon their bawling bugles. But of all the deeds of valor remembered from that day, the greatest belonged to Buffalo Calf Road Woman, who had gone along to tend the pony herd. When her brother had fallen from his mount, she had ridden up into the fire of the bluecoats and rescued him, a deed so courageous that the day would ever after be remembered as the Battle Where the Girl Saved Her Brother.

In this way one army of bluecoats had been turned back from the sacred land, but other armies were known to be on the march toward the Greasy Grass. To replace the ammunition spent in that fight at the Rosebud, Yellow Bird had returned the next day with the braves to search the battlefield for flattened bullets that might be melted down and recast into cartridges; these could then be reloaded. Better still, Yellow Bird had found handfuls of live shells scattered from the bullet pouches of the soldiers, and with the others he had filled several buffalo-calfskin sacks with them against the time when Sitting Bull's prophecy came to pass. When the last bullets had been gathered from the battlefield, a shallow grave was found and reopened. Bluecoat soldiers, abandoned in retreat, had been hastily laid there in their blankets. The blankets had been good still, once they'd shed the smell of white flesh, so the dead were rolled from them, and from their clothes as well, and they lay like a pile of limp white slugs for the vultures to devour. In the uniform pockets Yellow Bird had found the disks of yellow metal that drove the Wasichu crazy. They felt uncomfortable in his hand, as though they breathed and had a secret life of their own, and so he cast them away into the pools of the Rosebud River.

Seven days and eight nights had passed since the gathering of the bullets, and the bluecoat armies were drawing nearer to the Greasy Grass all the time. War was in the air, and so the boys played incessantly at fighting. They fired off arrows at leaves and buffalo chips, charged one another, hurled willow rods. There was no anger in it, and they all laughed, even he who was thrown down. As usual, Yellow Bird had no part in these games. He was different, and was envied for his real arrows. Most boys hunted with tips of wood, good only for stunning the smallest game.

This morning they were too many, too noisy, and most of the game had been frightened away. Yellow Bird, keeping to the fringe of the excitement, saw a prairie chicken. If he could get an arrow into the mother bird, the chicks would hop about her and could be finished off with a stick. Roasted over the coals, they were juicy morsels. The tougher hen could join his mother's wild turnips in the pot. But before he could shoot, the war game swung near, sending the quarry into cover. He kept on toward the river, hastening to keep ahead of the others, hoping to find a rabbit or another prairie chicken. The sage was gray and dusty where he walked, the grass dull red, already sun-weary, but beyond, where the red hills rose, the deep ravines were full of narrow creeks. There cottonwood grew thick, and the air was perfumed with aromatic pine and the scent of wild roses. Perhaps over on the other side there might be game. The water would be icy cold from the Big Horns, but shallow and with a slow current. It would be a satisfying escape from the blazing sun and the swarms of buffalo gnats against which he possessed no protective bear grease.

He was not the first to arrive at the river. Three braves were already there, swimming and shouting in a deep pool: William Yellow Robe, Wandering Medicine, and Charles Head Swift. They were all of his people. Some girls, their braids flopping down their backs, walked upstream, tearing the water with their kicking feet. The braves threw pebbles in their direction while the girls pretended the pebbles and the young men who threw them did not exist.

Yellow Bird put one foot into the water, and the cold took hold of him like eagles' talons. They would make fun of him if he drew back, and so he plunged in up to his knees, taking the pain. Ahead, the current ran thick and brown, whispering to him in a voice he could not understand. The surface was dimpled with yellow whorls like slow smoke from a grass fire. It was too thick to see through. There might be fish there, but one needed clear water to hunt with a bow. He had not brought the thread or the little hooks made from the ribs of a field mouse that were best for catching small fish. He pressed on into deeper, colder water, up to his aching chin before he felt sure he could wade to the opposite shore.

The sun stood high overhead as he gained the shore, but somehow its invitation had gone. The banks were steep, rock-strewn, and without appeal. The deep-cut watercourses led away to lonely strangeness, and he yearned for the camp, for the yipping yellow dogs and the safety of the great camp circle. Still, though human eyes were no longer upon him to judge his conduct, Yellow Bird proceeded up one of the dry washes. His bow was strung. The birds were silent. The water seemed to laugh at him. Something was coming, he felt it as surely as he had felt the coming of the thunder people in his dream. This time it was an enemy. He stood listening, then, stooping, drove his knife into the ground up to its hilt, to listen at the haft. Faint but sure he heard the round hoofbeats of many horses. Far away, stirring on the horizon like a pile of worms, was the great pony herd. But the herd was too far away for him to hear it, and there was something altered, more metallic in the sound that reached his ears. He stood up stiff as a dog on a scent while the blood rose to throb in his ears. Was it all childish fears? The braves still splashed in the river, unheeding. Was it his imagination? Ideas sometimes had come to him clear as audible voices.

Now he seemed to hear his mother calling him home. He wanted to run, but there was only the voice of the stream and the strum of cicadas from the trees warning him to flee. With his first returning step his apprehension grew, as real as a mountain lion crouched to spring. He ran from it, down to the riverbank and into the stream again, not feeling its icy grip this time. The braves saw him, noted his coming with a trifling pause, an exchange of glances, laughter. He was a child fleeing from shadows. He called to them, "Go back, go back!" All knew of the battle on the Rosebud, and many had mourned the slain. Many also heard the prophecies of Sitting Bull, that bluecoat soldiers would tumble into camp. Now that time had come, and the growing thunder of horses' hoofs suddenly stilled their laughter.

Yellow Bird stumbled into a deep pool, came up, choking, to be pulled along toward the bank by an older boy, Black Elk, an Oglala. For a moment they seemed to share alone a frightening secret, and then from the south there came a sound like buffalo grease snapping on hot coals. Guns were firing fast, and then the word was passed by hand signal, by lips, by the flashing of trade mirrors: "The chargers are coming! They are charging!"

Yellow Bird scrambled up the bank, the other children plunging before him. Braves ran by on either side. On higher ground he stopped, not knowing which way to turn. Black Elk stood beside him and pointed off to the south where the last tepees stood like a row of thorns. Dust boiled angrily above them. That was the Hunkpapa circle of Sitting Bull, and, as he had foretold, the bluecoats were falling upon it. Yellow Bird could tell no more from a distance, and it would be days before he heard the story of the first attack: how the bluecoats rode into camp firing at women and children, at anything that moved; how the family of Gall, the great war chief, was cut down in its lodge; and how Gall then rallied the Hunkpapa in his fury. "It made my heart bad," Gall would relate. "After that I killed the bluecoats with the tomahawk."

Yellow Bird felt sure he had heard his shrilling war flute; if not with his ears, then with his racing blood, a chilling call to slaughter. The braves had gathered in the south. They had rallied with their stone-headed clubs, their spears, trade muskets, and repeating Winchesters, to drive their attackers away. Stubbornly at first, the bluecoats had fallen back into a stand of timber. From there they had broken before the Indians, fleeing to the riverbank and down into the water. There the Indians found them, with bullets, arrows, bare hands, while Sitting Bull secured the sacred circle of the encampment against the second attack he had foretold. When the circle was free of living soldiers and when the riverbank was completely retaken, the women and children, sounding the tremulo, went out with knives and sticks to find the wounded, and punish the Wasichu for what they had done.

All this Yellow Bird would hear about later in story and song, but he had no time now to consider the tumult in the south, for across the river above the defile where he had gone to hunt there was more dust. It marked the ominous approach of bluecoats. Toward the river they came, the horses showing gray, the bugle flinging its piercing stutter, thin and brazen.

"Boots and Saddles" announced the slow advance of the Seventh Cavalry. One troop was mounted on reddish sorrels, another on grays, and the swallowtail guidon led the way. The column arrived at the ford where Yellow Bird had crossed. They were in the river now, splashing across. The three braves who had been swimming there waited on the far shore, just below where Yellow Bird stood transfixed. They had only bows and lances and they were singing their death songs as the troopers came on at a trot. Then four Cheyenne warriors led by Bobtail Horse came up with repeating rifles. Seven against an army.

Behind Yellow Bird, his people in the camp circle had reached the first full realization of disaster. Many appeared to be running in four directions at once. The criers were out shouting, "The soldiers are coming! Make ready! Your men are many and brave!" Boys were riding in with war ponies. A few women were striking their tepees. Dogs and children were howling underfoot. The Big Bellies bustled about dabbing on war paint and getting it all mixed up in their haste, while, like a blue steel blade, the column of troopers drove toward this hornet's nest.

The braves on the bank began firing. Rifles flamed from the river, and Yellow Bird could not hear the separate sounds any more; there was only one sound. A few more braves came up with flintlock trade muskets, aiming them high, for their bullets tired when they flew too far. In a minute they would all be overrun. Then one of the troopers whose jacket was buff, not blue, was hit. He slumped from his horse. Others gathered around, pulled him back into the saddle. The blue-coated riders milled about in midstream as the braves continued to fire and the war drums beat a steadier rhythm, filling the air with vibrations more felt than heard. "Better to die fighting . . . Better to die fighting . . ." they seemed to say. By now the war ponies were being brought in from the prairies. The braves were sorting out their weapons. They had donned war paint that was proof against fear—proof, they hoped, against wounds—and so they rode to battle. Many did not even ride their own ponies, for at such a time a warrior took the pony at hand. Should it die in the fight, its rider did not have to repay the owner, but whatever he might capture in the battle belonged to the owner of the pony he rode.

The dust rose around Yellow Bird as they galloped to the river. He yearned to be with them, but he had no horse to ride nor had he a weapon that could kill a man. Below, the bluecoats were turning back. Withdrawing up the defile, they fired one volley. Then they were gone, a smudge of drifting dust, appearing again, still mounted, on the Sacred Hill of the Wild Peas. The slope was in bloom, covered with pale pink and purple. The plants that the horses did not trample would ripen into buffalo beans and be picked by the women one day, but there was blood on them now as the troopers climbed the low hills. The warriors, for the most part stripped to their breechclouts, many unpainted, on foot, and without charms in their haste, stalked the soldiers up the draws and gulches near the river. When the bluecoats dismounted, seeking shelter behind boulders, volleys of arrows showered upon them. When they stood up, they were shot down. The Indian attack came on with shrill barking cries as the dust and confusion closed in.

Many were the strong heart songs that Yellow Bird heard sung that day. "Earth, have pity. Sky, see your sons. It is a good day to die." "Through many trials, my life is short." "It is bad to live to be old, better to die young." Over and over the braves went to battle, accepting death. Sioux and Cheyenne went together, the Sioux with their eagle-feathered bonnets, the Cheyenne with bonnets made of crow feathers; one people in this fight, the Sioux shouting their war cry, "Hoka-hey!" and the Cheyenne sounding like the crow, "Hey-hey-hey!" Some who rode had roped themselves to their ponies so that if they fell they would be pulled from the fight, but most approached the cloud of whirling dust on foot, not going recklessly, seeking no single glory, no bloodless coups, but fighting for the life of their people, meaning to kill or die.

Among the warriors who went to the battle of the Greasy Grass that day, among those who would either die or live to show their scars, there were many whom Yellow Bird recognized. Some he had been close to in the camp circles. Others he knew from the singing and praise of the old women, still others from the special paint and ornaments they wore. Wolf Tooth and Big Foot of his people passed. Then came Lame White Man, also of his people, wrapped in nothing but a blanket and steaming, for he had been caught in a sweat bath by the alarm. Scarlet Tip led the Santee braves. Among the braves was a Cheyenne woman, Moving Robe, who bore the staff of her brother, killed on the Rosebud. Horned and horribly painted, the shamans lined the riverbank and shook their medicine clubs toward the enemy.

Finally came the greatest of them all, up from the south. Yellow Bird could not mistake him. Crazy Horse sat his pony as though he had grown there. Not a tall man, Crazy Horse had a presence larger than that of other men, though his trappings were plain: buckskin shirt, dark-blue leggings, one feather in his long hair, the braids unbound and flying now that battle had come. When he rode hard, the fringed skin shirt flew about his shoulders like the wings of a bat. As he drew closer, Yellow Bird could see his paint, lightning streaks on his face, hailstone dots on his body. He was a breathing weapon. He could draw blood from the wind with his flung spear. "Only heaven and earth last long!" he shouted to the Dakotas who followed him. His pony reared, forefeet stabbing the air, and then he was down along the bank, drawing Cheyenne braves in his wake, for all men followed him.

Like a living arrow that grew in flight, Crazy Horse led his band far around behind the hills and the fume of battle. He would come up behind the crest upon which the bluecoats were making their stand. This Yellow Bird knew. They would not escape into the Big Horns, nor could they break through toward the Indian camp as they had first intended, for the fight was over in Sitting Bull's circle and Gall was gathering the Hunkpapa for a frontal attack. It came on like the leaping, raging waters from a cloudburst, and the bluecoats fell back before it, stumbling up the slope. Yet somehow the soldiers kept a straight line, making a dusty picture that Yellow Bird would remember in his singing, in his storytelling in years to come.

The firing never let up. The men fought in a fog of dust that hovered in sluggish clouds on the windless air. The braves moved toward it. Now and then saddled horses burst from the dust, some of them porcupine-quilled with arrows. Gray horses stampeded across the river. One still bearing its rider charged toward Yellow Bird. He let fly an arrow, and the horse shied, spilling its cargo. For an instant Yellow Bird thought he had done the impossible, laid low a six-foot trooper with an arrow fit only to hunt prairie chickens. It wasn't so. As he ran forward he noticed the great bullet hole in the trooper's body and the dark blood that oozed from it. Yellow Bird felt his breakfast turn in his stomach, and he did not go through the man's clothes as others would do. Neither did he take his gun, but near the corpse was a bright and beautiful thing. Like a yellow egg it was, and when he held it up he could hear its heart faintly beating. It lives, he thought. The thing was lidded, the catch sprung. Inside that lid was the tiny face of a Wasichu woman. She looks sad, he thought. She knows her man is dead. Soon her heart will stop beating, too.

Across the river, the fight must soon come to an end. Yellow Bird knew this, for the young braves were going in, those who had pledged themselves to suicide in the sacred ceremonies. It was a great thing to do, and yet, with the erupted flesh before him and the feasting flies, it did not seem as fine as it had the night before with the flames reaching up toward the black sky and the war drums pounding. As these young men went in bearing only knives and war clubs, more and more of the women came up toward the riverbank. Some sang the songs of victory already. Others keened for the dead, while a few avenged themselves on the bodies of the fallen bluecoats.

Before the firing had entirely stopped upon the Hill of the Wild Peas, the women were crossing the river. Yellow Bird's mother, Monahseetah, was among them. She had arrived silently and taken his hand, pressing it hard. She was tall and strong. She would have made a good warrior, Yellow Bird thought, and he did not hesitate to follow her across the river while others held back. Guns were still going off in the south. Many held back because of this, but Monahseetah and her son walked straight on as though they owned the ground beneath their feet.

They did not stop to deprive the dead of their ornaments. They did not take souvenirs, ears, noses, as many of the other women were doing, but headed straight for the crest where the last fight had taken place. Strange crowds rushed this way and that, riderless horses, braves carrying their dead and wounded home. Men staggered here and there as though filled with firewater, or sprawled in drunken heaps. A brave approached them, a wild picture of a man, sheathed in blood, his muscles fluttering with spent fury. With furious glee he held up a severed hand for them to see. That one would not shoot so well in paradise. Another passed displaying a blue shirt with the Seventh Cavalry insignia on the collar tab. "This day is my heart made good!" he shouted to them. It was the same insignia he had seen the day his wife and mother died, and so he was returning to camp crying out the news.

What Yellow Bird saw on either side as he climbed the Hill of Trampled Peas beside his mother was burned forever into his brain: scenes of great joy, of sorrow, of beauty and ugliness. The beauty of victory, the ugliness of pain and death. The joy of bravery and survival and the sorrow of the women finding their dead. Even the braves wept for their fallen friends as no bluecoat ever seemed to mourn his comrades. No hiding place remained for the stray soldier who still breathed. The women and their half-grown sons poked through patches of scrub and brush, setting the larger ones afire. From one such blaze Yellow Bird saw a bluecoat emerge, bounding like a jack rabbit, his hair afire. There was no way through the circle that surrounded him, but he went for it helplessly, head down, and the boys beat him to the ground with their bows. With nothing but their bows they killed him and stripped his body, which lay there naked and white as buffalo fat.

Another trooper feigned death, lay unmoving as two old squaws, fat as autumn cubs, stripped him of his clothes, coming to life with a roar only as they began to cut souvenirs from his body. A short blow of his fist flattened the nose of one squaw before they could collect themselves. Then they were upon him, bearing him down, as braves stood about roaring with laughter. They were on him with knives, knives held in the right hand with the fingers of the left hand gripping the right wrist to drive deep. For a moment the trooper pulled away, dragging himself backward on his elbows, knees flexing. "My God! Help me! God help me!" He rocked to and fro. His legs stretched. A fountain of blood poured from his mouth. Then the squaws had their souvenirs, among them a tattoo of an American flag that they took from his right arm.

Yellow Bird felt his stomach beating like a tom-tom. He wanted to be sick but knew others would laugh at him. He must harden himself to these things, to the flies and the sweet smell that grew in the heat. And then it was not all death and bloodshed. There was the throwing of the green paper into the air, small strips of paper with portraits of white men upon them. Some said they were pictures of the Great White Fathers in Washington. Some said that Squaw Killer, the one who led the bluecoats, wanted to have his face put on such paper, and so they cast it into the air for joy. They saved the ammunition from the saddlebags of the captured horses. That was more valuable than food. They saved the horses and the guns, and the clothing of the dead. One old war leader, Lame White Man, donned his blue coat too soon and in the confusion was mistaken for an Indian scout and killed.

Yellow Bird and his mother approached the final crest where the last of the bluecoats had been rubbed out. There the heat of the sun lay trapped like smoke beneath a blanket. Birds circled overhead, awaiting their turn. How harmless the Wasichu looked now, deprived of all their trappings, a ruin of dolls poured down from the sky as Sitting Bull had foretold, their chins blue and unshaven, their muscles knotted and lumpy, so unlike the smooth bodies of the braves.

Yellow Bird did not question why they went there. He did not know exactly what his mother was seeking, but he sensed immediately when she had found it, the naked body of a man. In no way was he special. His arms were flung out like the pictures in the book carried by the Black Robes. There was no wooden cross behind him, only a blue and bloodless wound sunk into his forehead like a knot into a tree. In death he was a small man with knobby knees, a hawklike face, and the red stubble of a beard upon his chin. The hair on his head was the color of frosty grass, and it was receding and thin. Not good enough for scalping. The braves had taken hair only from the Indian scouts.

"That is the one we call Squaw Killer," his mother told him. "I used to call him Pahuska, the Long-Haired One, but he is old now. He had eyes like iron that is wet." Now they were covered with flies.

"You know him, Mother?"

"Many winters ago. After the Washita. I knew him. I want you to hear me now, Pahuska," she said, "if your spirit is still in your body." She bent low, and taking a sewing awl from her pouch, she drove it deep into the dead man's right ear. There she stirred it around as though raising the meat in a pot of stew. Finally she withdrew the awl and spoke close to the un-hearing ear. "Now you will hear me better, Pahuska. You see this boy. You will never make a captive of him. Pahuska, this is our son."

So it was that Yellow Bird met his father after the battle recalled as Pehin Hanska Ktepi in the last days of the Moon of Making Fat. In the white man's reckoning it was June 25, 1876. The place was the Little Bighorn. The aging corpse that lay before them with the thinning hair and the fly-blown eyes was General George Armstrong Custer.

II

The Dull Knife Days

A strong smell of sage hung on the hot, still air as the sun set blood-red over the camp circles of the united peoples. Now he who had slaughtered Black Kettle and his tribe upon the Washita and made the Thieves' Road into the Black Hills was dead with all his men, and the deeds done this day would live in song and story long after none breathed who had witnessed them.

The remnant of those soldiers who had attacked Sitting Bull's camp in the south still held out on a hill across the river. After the short summer night they were attacked, but not by all of the braves. There was no pleasure or glory in crawling up a steep hill against men who had dug in. There was just heat and dust, hurting and death, with ammunition running low again, ammunition that they would need for hunting. Finally, rather than watch many braves die in a final assault, Sitting Bull called off the battle. "Henala!" he shouted. "Enough! The bluecoats wish only to live. Let them go. If we kill them too, a bigger army will march against us."

The People had had enough. There were dead to lament, wounded to heal, and heroes to honor. The Big Horns were masked in shadow with only their upper crests still iridescent when the last celebrations were begun. All the People took part—all, Yellow Bird heard, except Crazy Horse, who said the fighting had only begun.

Warriors, many of them with blue jackets thrown over their bone breastplates, rode two by two around the camp like soldiers. A bugle chattered and the women cried the greatness of the braves as they passed through the light of the campfires. Who could say if another war party like this would ever circle the camps? Only once before had such a camp been attacked, and that was long ago when Little Thunder was peace chief. This time they had scattered their foe like poisoned wolves upon the prairie, and Long Hair would never be the Great Father in Washington. Even the dead must be happy on the other side, for they had died like warriors.

In Yellow Bird's camp, the braves performed the shield dance with hawk bells jingling at their ankles, and the scalp dance too, in which the sacred buffalo hat was brought out. To the steps of the war dance, the braves stalked their enemy, crying out "Eeyah," and this time a real scalp was taken and it was well. The last of the bluecoat wounded had fallen into the hands of the widows and they had punished him, leaving two red holes beneath his brows. They had burned his body with hot coals from the fire, so that it was a kindness for the braves to let out his life. One of the braves even changed his name upon that occasion, carrying the bluecoat's naming with him forever after: Oh Mother.

Yellow Bird had seen the soldier give up his life. He had seen many do so in the last few days and it did not distress him, but in the roaring flames he saw things that made him afraid. There danced human forms that seemed to mock and beckon. "Your grandfathers are calling you," they seemed to say. They rode strange flaming horses with lightning and blizzards for manes, and white geese soared around them, glittering like the daybreak star. He saw the People, heads bowed, walking a mountain road. Their ponies were lean and famished, and the land offered only gray rock and the stumps of trees.

"What do you see?" an old woman asked him.

"Nothing. I see only the flames."

"There is more than that in your eyes, grandson," she told him.

He saw the bluecoats, too, marching, marching into the barren hills, and he became afraid and went away while the old woman looked after him. And though he could not see the fires any more, what they had revealed cast a pall between him and the bright star of victory, a pall that deepened with the dying of Chief Lame White Man. He was the only important Cheyenne chief to fall in the battle, and he was brought back from the hill to die with his people. There was a bullet inside him which felt better, he said, when it dropped into his stomach. The shaman tried to save him, even working a boiled cloth around in the wound as white men did, but the old chief passed into visions. He sees what I see, Yellow Bird thought, but he does not speak. And then the old man died and his relatives began the long lamenting: "Hownh, hownh, Lame White Man was a great chief and a friend, and now he is gone. Hownh." It was hard work lamenting, and thinking up what to say. Many made up songs. Some were about Long Hair, who would not return, and about his woman, crying, crying. When dawn came, his people wrapped the Cheyenne chief in his red blanket and erected his scaffold, painting it red and black, and much joy was gone from the camp.

Then the scouts returned and snuffed out the last of the

joy. More soldiers were coming, not cavalry this time but the "walk-a-heaps," moving slowly on foot and bringing with them the big guns which threw balls that burst like the sun. Should they stay and fight again? There was no one leader to tell them what to do. Ammunition was low. It did no good to ration out the powder, as some did, so that the bullets barely rolled out the end of the barrels. Then, too, there must be enough powder and shot left for the winter hunting. Crazy Horse, it was said, would fight with bows if need be, but Sitting Bull went out to the ridge where the battle had been fought and talked to Wakan Tanka. "Hear me," he said, "and pity me. I offer you this pipe in the name of my people. Save them. We want to live in peace. Guard them against all danger. Pity us." He stuck reeds into the ground to which were tied small buckskin sacks of willow bark and tobacco, on the same slope where he had placed them the day before Long Hair's troopers trampled them down.

When Sitting Bull returned to the camp, he said that he would move into the Paha Sapa, the Black Hills, the center of the world from whence the great directions ran to the corners of the earth. He did not command, but of course his people would follow him. And with Sitting Bull's going, the great camp began to break up. There was no haste, no panic. The horse soldiers, let alone the walk-a-heaps, could never catch them on the march. Yellow Bird and his mother struck their tepee that afternoon. They spoke little. It was something they had done a hundred times before. Each had his task. There was no change there and yet Yellow Bird sensed an enormous change, the end of one thing that was great and fine, and the beginning of something that was small and bad. What had happened so suddenly to victory? Why were they running away?

Yellow Bird held the nose rope of the broad, patient pony, which stood unmoving, head down, tail drooping, as his mother secured the travois poles. The warriors already were mounted, moving upriver. They rode slumped forward, the force gone out of them. In the years since Sand Creek, Yellow Bird knew, bad fortune had stalked his people. They were showing it now, on a day when moving should have been a joyous time of fun, with braves racing along the column, showing off their tricks for the girls, the women dressed in their best deerskin, fringed, beaded, faces vermilioned. It was not so this time. They went without song or laughter and the alkaline dust whirled around them.

The Cheyenne had the place of honor in the rear, just ahead of the braves who set fire to the grass behind them to screen their going. Yellow Bird and his mother were among the last to move. When the time came, Yellow Bird mounted the foreleg of the old pony as he would climb a tree. She knew when to move. Very little was left behind: a few dead horses, their legs pointing skyward like wooden pegs; the severed head of Bloody Knife, one of the bluecoats' Indian scouts; the body of Lame White Man. The soldiers would find these things and in time Lame White Man's polished skull would turn up in a Montana trading post, scrimshawed with the following legend: "I'm on the reservation at last."

For several days they moved, with bands breaking off to look for fodder and food, up along the emerald-green banks of the Tongue River, where the water was always clear and always cold: the tears of the Gods. By the Moon of Cherries

Ripening they were well into the hills, and their band had shrunk to those lodges which were under the leadership of Chief Dull Knife. They followed the Pumpkin Buttes, keeping them to the east with the old pipe-bearers going ahead looking for grass for the herd. Only in horses were they rich, for among their ponies now were big sorrels and bays that bore the 7USC brand.

For protection Yellow Bird and his mother stayed with Dull Knife's band, but they were not really part of it, never sharing in the feasts or in the games. They were tolerated as hangers-on and curiosities, but not welcomed. Rarely was Yellow Bird accepted in the sport of the other boys. He was used to that, as his mother was accustomed to never participating in the women's circle of gossip and the communal softening and preparation of hides for the coming winter. No adoptive set of parents was present to commiserate with Yellow Bird in times of trouble, or to take on his upbringing should his mother die. Hedged around by rejection, he and his mother had learned self-sufficiency.

Monahseetah was as vigorous as a brave, full of energy that burst from her skin, a straight walker, looking at no one but being looked at by the braves as her body moved under her light buckskin dress. They could do no more, for she had been a Wasichu's woman and no Cheyenne would have her as wife. Besides this taboo, there was a strangeness in her, not a madness or excitement, but the wildness of independence that went beyond the rules of decorum. She was inclined to sardonic laughter, seldom heard but always lurking in her dimpled cheeks. Monahseetah had hunted with a bow and a carbine when Yellow Bird was small. She still hunted with him, preferring in all things to do her own tasks without waiting for others. No one made better moccasins, cured meat that lasted longer, knew as many strong heart songs; she had even made up a few. She could find ripe berries or turnips when others came back empty-handed, and she butchered and cooked game fast and well whether it was mouse or moose.

This self-sufficiency Monahseetah expected in Yellow Bird. She was no coddler, and he found out about such things as glowing coals, not by a warning but by feeling the fire's bite. At the same time, he knew that if the occasion demanded, if a grizzly bear appeared at the tent flap, Monahseetah would die fighting with a knife in her hand before Yellow Bird was scratched. Nor was she all toughness, but a sweet songstress, carrying a melody soft and warm in her throat. Her singing was unlike the singing of the People. It was something she had borrowed from the whites, but in the process she had changed the result so that there seemed nothing left in it for him to hate.

Best of all, she was a storyteller. "Tell me of the old days, before the white man came," was how their evenings usually began during the quiet time in the mountains after the battle on the Greasy Grass. His mother would throw her mind back to the times before the withering of the sacred tree, when the four-leggeds and the two-leggeds lived together as brothers. Her tales lived in Yellow Bird's brain, more real than memory. He could see the sacred tree in flower and the circle of the nation's hoop, endless, unbroken, and powerful. His people walked the red road then.

"You have heard of Winio, the Wondrous One," she would begin, "who went too far in all things. You have heard of his magic sack full of buffalo, and how he opened it too wide and freed the herds that trampled him to death but gave us food forever. You are too old, my son, for that story now. It is a toy for children to play with. And I have told you, too, of the times when your people lived in the forests until the Chippewa took trade guns from the white man and pushed us out into the great plains where your grandfathers fought the Pawnee and Shoshoni and Crow in the old way with bows and feathered clubs. In those times, when a brave ran out of arrows he had to stand fast for one to be returned. He might have to pluck it from his own flesh. In this way steel arrow tips came to us." Monahseetah spoke solemnly, for the tales were great and true, and her listener should become greater through hearing them.

"What I will tell you now is about your grandfather, Black Kettle, and how your father killed him. All this was after the great sickness, and after the time of the first wagons. The Wasichu had fought a great war in their own land, so their soldiers had gone away, but the wagons came and the singing wire that our people cut down to hear the song. Then, after the bluecoats stopped warring among themselves, came the iron road. We knew little of the white man then, and even less of his strange powers. There was a brave who tried once to throw a noose around the neck of an iron horse and bring it home."

"Did he put a rope around it?" Yellow Bird asked.

"He did," she told him. "A very strong rope."

"Did the iron horse follow him home?"

"No." She seemed to be laughing now. "It ran away with him. He wouldn't let go, and so it dragged him until his arms were broken. That is the old one they called Crippled Wing. He was very brave and very foolish, but we knew nothing about the white man in those days. Black Kettle, your grandfather, was like that. He believed the white man meant well, that he would move on, that the land was big enough for all. So he gave away our land and we were massacred not one time, but twice, by the bluecoats, and for this they call him a diplomat among our people."

"A diplomat?"

"That is a word the Wasichu use. It means fool." Her tone was harsh, which seemed odd, for Yellow Bird knew how much she still loved her father, whom he had never known.

"Tell about Black Kettle," Yellow Bird urged.

"I will not speak again of Sand Creek, where your grandfather flew the Wasichu flag with the stars above his lodge in a sign of friendship. The bluecoats came in the night. In spite of that flag, they attacked and murdered our people until the river ran red with killing and the rising sun. I was a girl then. I agreed with my father that we should not fight back. We ran away to the hot land where they do not dress as we do. They wear cloth blankets and leggings traded from the white men. They made fun of our buffalo robes and buckskin. We had trouble talking. Our words were like the Sioux and theirs like the Apache.

"Four times," she continued, "the buffalo grew his winter coat after the Sand Creek, and I was a woman. By this time, my father had led us to the valley of the Washita. There was trouble again with the white soldiers. My father wished to meet with them and speak of peace. The braves in council did not talk against him, but they were angry, and only to me he said, 'Daughter, I am of two hearts. Since the white man killed my people and burned our tepees, it is hard to believe him. But what can I do? For every flake of snow that strikes this lodge, there is a bluecoat. How can we fight them?' I could give him no answer.

"I went to sleep without helping him. It was snowing. I remember the Moon of Falling Leaves was over and it was the Time of Popping Trees. Your grandfather rose early to see how much snow had come. I followed him outside. The sky was clearing, but there was low fog. I could see the high ridges above the river, and just before the morning star of wisdom faded, there came a strangeness in the sky. It was like a great ball of flame changing color from red to yellow, then from green to blue. Black Kettle said it was the rainbow bridge which braves rode in glory to the other world, that few men were privileged to see it while they lived. It was a good thing, he said. He was wrong. I remember how still it was in the fog along the river. Then a dog barked, and we heard the bluecoat music, that which they call 'Gary Owen.' Our people began to run from their lodges. 'Soldiers! Soldiers!' they shouted. Your grandfather came with his rifle. He could not believe it. Sand Creek was happening again. He wanted to stop the soldiers. He mounted his pony. I leaped up behind him and hung on with my arms around his body. We rode until the bluecoats came out of the mist. My father raised his hand in the peace sign. My hands were still locked around his body when the first bullet struck him. He raised his right hand again to show he had no weapon, and once more they shot him. We fell into the snow and then the bluecoats rode over us.

"Later they came back. They pried my fingers from him one by one and carried me to a corral full of our people. Some were wounded. Some sang their death songs with their hair undone and their blankets up over their faces. We waited until the Wasichu leader came. His Indian scouts called him Hard Backsides. After this time they called him Son of the Morning Star for what had happened in the sky. That was your father, Yellow Bird, the one whose name was Custer. I remember his eyes. They were like two nailheads hammered into his face."

"Is this when they shot the ponies?" Yellow Bird interrupted. Somehow that was the worst.

"No, they burned the lodges," she went on, "so there would be no shelter for those who escaped into the snow. Then they shot the ponies. At first the men would not do it, and your father raged at them. His voice was thin and cold as the blade of a knife. When they did not begin the shooting, he used his pistols. He shot the stray dogs, too, and because he was angry and his pony was bucking, he shot one of his own dogs by mistake, a huge beast the Wasichu called a staghound. After that no man dared question his orders. A firing party drove the big herd round and round, shooting them until the trampled snow was red as sunset. All this your father marked down on paper and, when it came to his own staghound, I was told he wrote, 'Shot by Indian arrows in the line of duty; alas, poor Blucher.'

"When the killing and the burning were finished, he came to the corral where we were held. He wanted an interpreter," explained Monahseetah. "He wanted me, although I did not speak his tongue."

"I have not heard this part before," interrupted Yellow Bird, though he had known, since seeing the body of the white chief and hearing her speak of him, that things he might not want to learn were coming.

"No, but now it is time. I was young. I had a good face. Do you wonder why I did not fight? Why I did not say no? The other women pushed me. Even my father's sister pushed me, saying it would be a great honor. I was young and afraid, and so I went with him though I could not speak English. Hear me, I became his woman. I was his woman until the Moon of Black Cherries, but even then I could not get used to his smell."

"I have never smelled a white man, not a living one," Yellow Bird said.

"He smells little, but what he smells like is death. I went with him to the camps of the Cheyenne and I talked to the keeper of the sacred arrows. It is what my father would have wanted, since there was no game for our people, and before the Snow-Blind Moon, when winter was old, the people surrendered at Fort Cobb. By that time I knew I was with child. I was afraid. It was a great thing, some said, to take the power of these white men who had no women of their own. Such a child would be strong among the People, they said. When I told your father, he just looked at me. He said nothing, but when we started back to the fort in the spring, he told me he had one wife and wanted no more. For this I shed no tears. I wished to be back with our people, and outside the fort I was turned over to the stockade guards. They put me with Cheyenne people who were prisoners. In the dust of the Moon of Black Cherries, you were born there. You were born with yellow hair, and I held you up in both hands and said to the four corners, 'They will not have this one. He shall never belong to the Wasichu.'

"Afterward, when we were let go, we went north. You rode in a cradleboard, the one that still hangs there on the lodgepole. Later you went on a pony drag. You rode with the old woman who is dead now, my father's sister. At night when you wanted to cry I had to put my hand over your mouth.

You can't remember, but you learned to be silent. I never punished you as whites punish their children."

"Do you not hate the white man?" he asked her. Surely she had better reason than he, and he hated them: hated them in the reflection he saw in the cracked trade mirror, the thin nose, the light eyes tinged with gold, the hair streaked with silver. He tried once with both hands to yank out the fair strands until tears of rage had stood in his eyes. It was useless. The hair was part of his name, in his blood, part of him forever.

"I do not like the white man's ways, but they are men."

"They try to drive us from the sacred land."

"Would we not do the same, if we were many and they were few?"

"Would we be outcasts?"

"Listen," said Monahseetah, "I will tell you of Unktomi, the fool and trickster." Unktomi was in all the old for-fun stories but when Monahseetah told of him, he was always white as things found under stones. Only through these stories heard by Yellow Bird during the late summer of the year when Long Hair Custer was killed did he learn of his mother's life among the white men, and only gradually did he realize how alone she had been then and afterward. And once, never to be repeated, after a day of futile hunting when they both returned bone-tired and hungry, he put his arm around her, seeking consolation, and discovered from the convulsive movement of her body that she was sobbing without a sound. At the touch of his hand she became still. "Tomorrow," she said. "Tomorrow we will hunt again."

Summer was already old. The big buffalo herds had begun to gather and the bulls to fight over the cows. It was a time to hunt and store up food for the winter to come, but they camped high above the realm of buffalo and could expect only deer or antelope. Because of the quickness of these animals and because even here the white man might be near, they kept to the great trees. Yellow Bird loved the woods. He owned none of the land, wished to own none, in fact did not even speculate upon the possibility any more than he would consider owning the wind or the sunshine. The earth belonged to no man, and in the breeze-stirred branches he heard the muttering of ancestors trying to address him in whispers. Sometimes, while waiting in hiding, he would listen for hours, waiting for the trees to break their mysterious silence, but their murmuring was always in a strange tongue.

On this occasion he and his mother followed a mountain stream looking for a watering place, then followed a wolf's trail in hopes that it would lead them to game. There were more wolves than ever this year, thanks to the many buffalo carcasses the white hunters left upon the plain, and the small game was vanishing well before the frost. The trail led along a narrow river belted with cottonwood. At each step they sank deep into the carpet of dead leaves. They made no sound, and so were able to creep up on a herd of antelope, close enough to risk a shot. Then underfoot a twig snapped, and as one the rumps of the antelope flashed white, a signal of alarm, and they were gone. A black-tailed deer appeared in the distance, then drifted away, and in the end they had to settle for a jack rabbit, which Yellow Bird turned in its upward bounding flight and sent tumbling downhill, head over tail, more dead from falling than from Monahseetah's bullet. Boiled with prairie onions, it was no worse than other things Yellow Bird had tasted. But it was buffalo he craved, the feasting and the excitement.

Most of all, he longed once again to see the great herd. Long ago he had seen it, in the summer of the grasshoppers that had darkened the sky. He had thought nothing could be so awesome as that storm of insects until he had seen the buffalo, that older race ruled over by the white buffalo god. At first there had been only a thickening of the horizon, and then that fuzzy blur had pulled free of the sky. "Hear them," his mother had whispered. He had not needed to stick his knife in the ground, for their hoofs rumbled as though from deep within the earth. The valley had been as long as a man could walk in a day and they had filled it, a living black river full of subterranean thunder. Then the hunters had ridden out to mill the herd and shoot them down. His part had come with the butchering, a time of giddy, gory joy, a time for gorging. Saliva filled his mouth at the memory, and he could have eaten an entire carcass right down to the hoofs.

Now, with game running short in the Moon of Cherries Ripening, it was decided to risk encountering the white soldiers. A buffalo hunting party of younger braves agreed to go out. The braves smoked solemnly with Dull Knife, and then burst from his camp, whooping around the drumming, singing camp circle. As they rode off, Yellow Bird knew that he and his mother would be the last to profit from their kill, but it was good to see and hear gaiety once more. It did not last long. There was an anxious time of waiting, and then the hunters returned with no game to speak of, only the shreds of an old bull, nearly too tough to eat. They'd come across moldering bodies left by the white men, fit only for wolves and coyotes, but they had many tales to tell. The only good thing that had happened was finding a Wasichu shepherd with a flock of those foolish white creatures who made themselves tame for the white man. They'd watched for a while, amusing themselves, and then descended, shouting and banging their shields, so that the shepherd and his flock had stampeded into a lake. The sheep in their excitement had tried to walk on each other's backs.

That was their funny white man. There had been others. They had run across gold hunters, the Big Horners, men so evil not even the white fathers wanted them around, the sort who would shoot a stray Indian just to keep blood bad. They'd exchanged shots once or twice. They had killed a black man, and regretted it afterward because the gun he had pointed at them turned out to be a broomstick darkened with axle grease. They had seen Indians, too, and heard rumors of Sitting Bull heading north, of Crazy Horse raiding miners in the hills, and of soldiers marching. Worse, there was talk of the loafer Indians, the crackers and molasses Sioux, who no longer loved freedom but who hung around the white man's agency living on handouts. They were being pressured into signing away the Black Hills. Some said Red Cloud, who had once defended the sacred land, now in his dry-voiced age had already signed, and that Spotted Tail and other submissive chiefs were following his example.

All this seemed but talk, the imaginings from another world, to Yellow Bird, until he saw the dust streamers of soldiers beyond count, their horses and their big-mouthed guns heading into the sacred Paha Sapa, toward that spot where the hoop of the world bent to the four directions. Dull Knife's band was too few to fight them, but the Cheyenne women stood strong beside their men. They would not run, and so it was decided to fire the prairie grass to make food scarce for the big-bellied horses of the Wasichu. Yellow Bird was not invited to go along, but there was no time in life when such things were forbidden, and no one to say no when a boy had made up his mind. Monahseetah went as well, and the braves talked to her as though she were another brave.

The prairie grass was still too green with summer to burn well, and the smoke was heavy and yellow, throwing misty screens up to hide the sun. Later, when the dry wind came from the north, the fires ranged higher, and Yellow Bird watched them with wide-open eyes and found them beautiful. The smoke drove as low as fog above a river, then leaned against the gusts from the mountains and rose into great white towers. The pillars of smoke by day became pillars of fire by night, and the dull pulsating roar of flames as they leaped from his smoldering brand into the tall grass seemed to whisper a message just beyond understanding.

So they burned the prairies, eluded the horse soldiers, and found what game they could while the Moon of Cherries Ripening became the Moon of the Black Calf and katydids throbbed louder under the leaves. Then another moon stood in the east, thin as a drawn bow. The cold moons were at hand and an autumn breeze hummed through the dry grass. Now the high forests were aglow as birch and aspen turned yellow and gold. Their leaves were fired from within, as if they had pulled down some radiance from the lagging sun.

With all their burning of the grass, the Indians were still being hunted by the soldiers in the Big Horns when the buffalo berries were frost-sweetened on their gray bushes. Yellow Bird and his mother knocked the fruit down with sticks for winter eating. The chokeberries bent low under their dark and shining plumes of fruit, but it was meat they needed, and meat they could not find. There had been much hunting of game and drying of meat for the summer fighting, but now the supply was low. Yellow Bird counted out their black jerked buffalo strips, cut so thin that flies could not blow them, and guessed they had only enough to last through the first snows.

Another hunting party was planning to go out, and this time Yellow Bird intended to ride with it, taking his bow. Monahseetah would carry the gun, for she was still the better shot, but these plans were changed as soon as they were made by a scout who had found his way from Slim Buttes on Rabbit Creek. He came with news as sad as death, news that had to be told true after the smoking of a sacred pipe. So it was first told to the Big Bellies and then cried about the village. The secret camp of Iron Shield, whom some called American Horse, had been found by the bluecoats, though it was hidden by steep bluffs. The stampeded pony herd gave the alarm and the braves had time to arm themselves before the attack. It was not to be another Sand Creek or Washita. The Sioux withdrew in good order. Only Iron Shield, a few warriors, and some women and children were cut off in a cave. Two hundred rifles poured a ricocheting fire upon them while the trapped women sang their death chant. The fight went on for hours.

Then Iron Shield came out walking stiff and straight, one hand holding his gun, the other spread wide over his lower abdomen to keep his intestines from falling out. An army surgeon looked him over and said he would surely die. Iron Shield took the news and the pain calmly, and sat by a fire with his blanket wrapped about him until the time came.

Meanwhile, his village was put to the torch by the bluecoats. When the white soldiers found Seventh Cavalry horses among the Sioux pony herd, nothing was spared, and the smoke made a heavy choking fog in the valley, through which only the bright flashes of rifle fire could be seen when Crazy Horse arrived on the bluffs above. He came too late, with too few. The bluecoats drove him away, losing in the process one of their Indian scouts named Charley White Buffalo, who liked to call himself Bill Cody when the real Cody was away.

As Dull Knife's people heard the terrible story, they knew it could as easily have happened to them. Gloom settled over the encampment. They felt defeated, without having fought. It was only in the old stories that the enemy always lost. The braves, who were glorious in victory, now felt downcast and confused.

"If the bluecoats come here, will we fight them?" Yellow Bird asked.

"Some will fight," Monahseetah told him. "Some will surrender. Many would go to the agencies now, if they could, for the food."

"What will we do?"

"We will stay. We will stay as long as anyone."

"I have heard the Wasichu kills his enemy by dropping him with a rope around his neck to seal his soul in his dead body like rotten meat in a sack."

"I have seen that done to a bluecoat," she replied.

"Have you seen the big guns that shoot twice, once from the gun's mouth and again when the bullet strikes? Does the Great Spirit make it do that for his white children?"

"He is a cruel god. It would be just like him," she said. "Now sleep. Tomorrow the camp will move."

The tepees were struck before dawn. A safer place had to be

found. Scouts rode ahead looking for messages left in pictures along the sand of riverbanks, for the shod hoofprints of the bluecoats' horses, consulting the freshness of campfire ashes, always looking for some secret valley where they might be safe for the winter. Sometimes the enemy was so near they had to hold their ponies' noses to keep them from whinnying. At other times, in the thick pine forests just below the first snows where the streams cascaded over great rocks and the lakes were blue as though they had fallen from the sky, they seemed to be the only living people on the face of the earth. But time was running out, for with the Moon of Water Freezing had come more bad news, which made some of the People desert and head for the agencies.

The agency Indians had indeed sold the sacred Paha Sapa, the Black Hills, to the Wasichu. They had sold them even though Crazy Horse's envoy, Little Big Man, had appeared at the council and promised to kill any chief who spoke of selling. So it was done on paper, and so the first snow fell and melted, fell again and melted, and finally fell to stay on the ground, with the drifts beginning to build.

These were hard times for the ponies. They were thin already from an autumn on the run, and the valley's thick grass as much as anything else made Dull Knife and his Big Bellies decide to stay. The winter camp was a good one, less than an arrow's flight from one side of the camp circle to the other. It was set amid green-black cedar and jack pine, so that one had to be almost directly above the camp to see it at all, and when the morning fog rose over the river, it was lost from sight entirely. The settling down brought a renewal of gaiety to the people. In the morning the women went in small groups for wood. Laughing and telling stories, they walked single file through the shallow snow while the men and boys broke open the thin ice on the stream to search in the deeper pools for the dormant fish. For good health and to wash away sickness, many went bathing through the ice.

Yellow Bird and his mother set up their tepee at the closed end of the valley. The hides of their lodge were growing thin with age and use. At night, with a fire inside, it glowed like a paper lantern. He could recognize his mother from her shadow cast on the skins. The other tepees were just as worn, and the whole camp circle shone like a great necklace of tawny beads. How beautiful it was with the snow and the tall black trees behind it, and then the mountains rising up, becoming a part of the lowering sky. Yet, without being able to tell himself why, Yellow Bird loathed the place. If the choice were his, he would run back and strike the tepee and head deeper into the hills, for it seemed as though something were stalking them, stalking all the time with a hateful heart.

The next morning Yellow Bird rose early. He had decided to try his luck fishing with a spear through the broken ice. Stepping from the animal warmth of the tepee into the wintry darkness was like walking into a knife. There had been snow during the night and it had encrusted the trees and bushes, painted the ground. Such a surface took a footprint and there were none ahead of him as he set out for the stream. He wore moccasins, and his feet crunched the brittle grass down. A couple of camp dogs followed him, their breath steaming around his legs. Otherwise it was quiet, quiet as when the frost is forming. The only other creature abroad was a hooded owl, devouring its prey in a tree. As he passed, it dropped a scattering of small bones.

"If you are trying to tell me something," he said, "I don't

understand you, owl." The owl gazed down at him, round eyes bright, then veiled as though a shutter had been drawn.

The stream was deserted, and the holes frozen over from the day before. He cracked one open with a stone. Then he waited, the spear point poised above the slow, oily flow of the stream. The water below remained clear, dark, and empty. He waited, not even hearing the approach of the old squaw man Plenty Lice, a loner and a visionary, whose visions never collected themselves sufficiently to make him able as a shaman, whose memory was too vague for him to be the tribal bard. He was just a laughed-at hanger-on at the council fire who slept out more than he slept in. His lips were chapped so badly in consequence that he dared not laugh, let alone smile.

That had been a game for days, to crack old Plenty Lice's lips with laughter. No one had succeeded, and he watched solemnly now, waiting for Yellow Bird to make his first cast. Yellow Bird threw once at a shadow and missed. By then the sun was climbing behind the mountains. It flamed in the mist, with that odd mixture of splendor and regret which Yellow Bird always felt at dawn or dusk. By the time he made his second cast, women were hurrying to the stream for water, for they could not use the dead water that had stood through the night. The second cast was a hit and the spear was almost jerked from his hands. Taken by surprise and afraid of losing his only spear, Yellow Bird stepped forward into the hole, landing waist-deep in water that gnawed through his leggings as sharp as wolves' teeth, piercing to the bone. He was out in a second, dancing about with the pain of it, while old Plenty Lice barked with laughter like a dog, though his lips cracked and the blood ran down.

Despite the needling water, Yellow Bird had to laugh back at the old Indian on the bank, who was now holding a hand to his mouth. Yellow Bird laughed for Plenty Lice and his chapped lips; he laughed for his fish, a big one. He kissed its cold scales so that its spirit would not return to the stream with bad words about him. Then he started for home, the morning breeze setting talons to his legs. Frost prickled all over his body till he yearned for the fire, for Monahseetah's pleasure at his catch, and for the smell of the fish roasting on the coals.

He still had a long way to go when that bright, brassy, most hated of sounds stuttered and squealed through the golden mist, a bugle accompanied by a cry like the passing of a flock of southbound geese, the Pawnee war cry. It was an attack.

The fish was forgotten. Yellow Bird, clenching his spear in both fists, made a stumbling, numb-legged run for his lodge. The Pawnee mercenaries had already ridden once through camp on their fleet ponies as the people ran out into the snow, many of the braves naked except for their guns and cartridge belts. Behind the Pawnees came the soldiers, more carefully, picking their targets.

The tepee was ahead, across an open space. Yellow Bird knelt down under the cover of the pines. He took a long, slow, lung-stabbing breath and then ran out through the singing bullets. Something scalded across his arm, but he dared not fling himself down for fear he would not get up again. Before he could dive into the tepee itself, a horse and rider intervened. The horse rose high, seeming to hang over him with its hoofs, and above the thrashing hoofs a saber glinted like the first silver shaving of a new moon. Then both horse and rider came down. He felt surprise more than pain. He had been hit, and the darkness closed around him.

He awoke from painful nightmares at what seemed only a moment later. The light was the same, but there was frost on his arms and on his face, and the body of a horse lay across his legs. Clearly a day and a night had passed. The slowly cooling horse had kept him alive through the cold. He was not trapped by the horse nor were his legs broken, but there was a deep slash across his left arm that oozed when he stood up. For a plaster, he urinated onto a patch of dry ground, and with the mud he covered the open wound. Then, stiff and aching, he renewed the short journey that he had begun the day before. There were no lodges now, but only frost-covered lumps: two-leggeds, four-leggeds, and round black rings of ruin where the tepee had stood. In the first such charred circle he found Plenty Lice, flung across still-glowing coals, but in death his seamed lips grinned merrily as though the secret that for so long had eluded his cluttered brain had finally revealed itself. There were many dead. Most of the women had their dresses pulled up over their heads.

Monahseetah, when he found her, was not this way. She sat cross-legged before the remains of her lodge. There was a carbine in her lap, the one with which she must have shot down the horse and rider who had meant to trample and slash her son. "Mother," he cried, running to her, "you are living." She did not reply. She did not raise her eyes, which were fixed on the ground. "Mother!" He touched her shoulder, and she leaned forward toward him, collapsing slowly at the waist. From the back of her head, as though casually lodged in a log of wood, protruded a Pawnee tomahawk, and in those astonished wide-open eyes, now glazed with frost, he seemed to see the reflected flames of rapine and massacre.

Nothing remained, nothing in this world for which he cared. Great chasms seemed to open around his feet and he felt himself plummeting through gray and empty space. The grief that held him was beyond tears, beyond thought. He might have stood there unmoving until the blood congealed in his veins but for a few of the people who returned from hiding to find relatives and to salvage what they could. They made a fire to warm him and forced him to eat. From their lips came the tale. A young brave, Beaver Dam, had betrayed them to the bluecoats. Now his name was accursed. Even betrayed and taken by surprise, the braves had fought well. Dull Knife had rallied them upon the upper slopes, finally driving the bluecoats and their Pawnee allies away. In the fight Dull Knife had lost his favorite son, and the loss had broken his spirit. With many of the other survivors, he had set out for the Red Cloud agency to surrender to the white men.

Those who had broken with Dull Knife were the tough, hard fighters, those for whom the sacred hills were as important as life. They meant to take their women and children and join Crazy Horse. Yellow Bird would go with them, they told him, and he answered neither yes nor no, not caring: not caring that his stomach was empty, his arm aching, or the weather growing colder and promising more snow. The following morning they set out. Ponies were few. Robes and blankets were mostly salvaged from the ruins, charred and full of holes. Some lacked even moccasins and trod the frozen ground barefoot.

That night the old man of the north sent the wind and the killing cold. So that the small children would not die, half of the ponies were slaughtered and disemboweled. The children were then thrust inside the still-warm bodies. The elderly people shoved their hands and feet in with the children. Yellow Bird tried for no such accommodation and he would most certainly have lost fingers and toes in the night from frostbite if one of the squaws—a little, bent, infinitely old woman, with a face roughhewn as from dark wood and hands that suggested an eagle's heritage—had not forced him down beside her. They sat close together throughout the destroying windy night. When dawn came, despite all their efforts, seven of the children were dead. Five more would die the next day, though the temperature rose.

Yellow Bird had not eaten. His stomach did not remind him of this, but he felt it in his limbs. They were weak beyond sensation. He walked lightly as though on a summer cloud, and he was only dimly aware of people straggling out ahead of him, black floundering lumps against the white glare of winter. By afternoon of that third day the glare was gone. Clouds had piled up on the warming wind and toward dusk it began to snow.

III

Son of Worm

They were not up to another fight. They were forlorn and beaten, a last remnant cut to the bone. When a message arrived that the bluecoats' Pawnee scouts were on their trail, one brave went back, his revolver loaded with six bullets, the powder behind each one barely sufficient to propel the lead from the barrel. With this he was expected to hold off the Pawnee until the snow obscured the trail. It was falling fast now and footprints were devoured soon after they were made. One shot was heard, another, and then no more. The brave was not seen again, nor were the Pawnee trackers. Visibility vanished when the wind rose at dusk. The horsemen, the mountless braves, their women, some with the grim bundles of their frozen babies, walked into it, always into the wind, not daring to stop.

Yellow Bird lagged behind. He felt the chill of the northern void sinking to his bones. He was alone, without kin. Even the old woman who had saved him the first night had disappeared, and as he moved one leg after the other he dreamed first that the pulse that beat in his head was a small drum; tum te tum, tum te tum, it sent its message of life. Only gradually did he become aware that no one walked ahead, and no one behind. Snow muffled his first shout, then melted in his mouth. He kept going for a while, remembering that he had seen his first white men in the snow. They had been in a stagecoach shaped like an egg. U.S. MAIL in gold letters had been written on the side, and it had been mired up to the wheel tops in drifts. Four mustangs had been under the snow, frozen stiff, good meat at a time when there was no other. The passengers had sat inside like figures cut in milky marble, three men and one woman. Peering through the frosted glass, Yellow Bird had expected them to scream at the sight of him, but they were immovable. Their serenity was eternal, and he had felt their glacial chill in his veins. So they were mortal, after all, those Wasichu. The knowledge had been reassuring on the one hand, but, upon reflection, disappointing, since it seemed they had achieved no better understanding of death than his own people.

It was colder now than it had been then. Yellow Bird could no longer feel his legs and arms, but there was a hot pain deep in his chest. Only when he had concluded he was lost did he see a figure moving ahead of him. He followed it, half blind now, and not until he was passing beneath trees where the storm was abated did he recognize the smoky plume ahead of him. He was following a wolf. It looked back, saw him, and went on without haste. The wolf is my four-footed brother, he told himself. So he followed to where great boulders leaned together, forming a cave. The wolf entered. Yellow Bird followed, not caring if it turned on him in defense of its lair. But it had already vanished into the cave's deeper recesses, back where rattlesnakes were inclined to hibernate during the winter. He collapsed near the entrance. Above him on the rock walls were paintings of buffalo with braves chasing them.

The storm wind yanked at his hair, and Yellow Bird rose to move farther back into the cave. He felt weightless in midstride and fell flat, though he thought he was still walking as he lay face down. He was following a long red road toward a rainbow through summer plains full of buffalo and quiet lodges and people who waved to him as he passed. At one village, people and four-leggeds danced together for joy around a sacred tree, a tree not stripped and dead like the sun-dance pole but rich with heavy green branches and singing birds. He went on and on, and people followed him. They were well fed, their ponies were fat, and behind them, like a trailing fog, came the ghosts of his grandfathers, going back further than the stories. Over them all arched the rainbow bridge, and beyond, stitched with lightning and made of cloud, was the sacred tepee.

It was just up the cloudy road now, its flap thrown open invitingly. He was about to enter when he felt himself being shaken, forced back reluctantly into the watery light of dawn. He struggled, helpless as a rat in a dog's jaws, then felt himself lifted and cast down across the back of a pony. A rider was up behind him, commanding his mount as though the two of them were of one piece. Drifting in and out of consciousness, Yellow Bird saw the sacred lodge again. He saw a face with broad cheeks, deep-set eyes, a strong nose. It had the strength of dull, hammered bronze that showed the tool marks still. He heard a low vibrant voice. "Now, grandson, you don't want to act this way before the braves. They, too, are tired. What will they think of you, coming into camp like a sack of white man's flour?"

Yellow Bird managed to prop himself up and strange hands steadied him. The real world was coming back, and he hung onto it grimly. He saw tepees ahead, tree-sheltered and piled around with drifted snow.

"My lodge is yours," a man's voice told him, and he was helped down and into the nearest tepee. In the center glowed a fire of buffalo chips. With the first warmth Yellow Bird became aware of the smell of cooking venison and the aroma of the black medicine that the white man called coffee. Like a long-legged spider, hunger crawled through his stomach until the strange hands put one and then the other to his lips. He gulped down food and drink together like a starved dog, scalding his throat. The heat flamed through him, spinning him away into oblivion while outside the wind hummed and whistled. When Yellow Bird finally waked from deep sleep, he sat up in confusion, seeing before him a bluecoat soldier. He tried to rise, but the soldier put hands upon him, holding him down. "No," he said, "I will take care of you. You may speak to me as your father."

"My father is dead," Yellow Bird told him. He was still suspicious, but he saw now that it was only an old man clad in a blue officer's coat, ventilated by crickets and stiffened with grease.

"Many are," the old man replied. "You may speak to me as though I were your father. My name is Worm."

The old man who called himself Worm had a cascade of clean white hair that framed a flinty face, tattooed here and there with battle scars. His whole body was scarred and worn, but not weakened by the years so much as toughened, as a tree clinging to a cliff edge will become hard, turning an ax until the day it falls. In many ways he resembled such a tree. His flesh was like dry leaves, his hands knotty and tough as roots. His teeth were missing except for one long yellow fang in front and a set of dark-brown grinders on the left side, the only spot where he could bite or really chew. The overall effect was strange and might have been frightening but for the eyes. Set deep in that dark, fierce face, they were wise and gentle.

"Grandson, I don't think you like my name," Worm said, smacking his palms against his knees and shaking with amusement. "Then you will call me Grandfather."

Worm was not the tepee's only occupant. The warrior who had found him at the cave was gone, but there was a woman seated near the fire. She was not a maiden, nor was she very old. Even wrapped in her blanket, her form lacked the sturdy thickness of a thoroughly married woman. Yet someone surely loved her, for her cheeks were vermilioned and her braided hair was wrapped in weasel fur. The scarf she wore was a thing of great wonder. It was made of the old-time sea shells brought from beyond the western mountains long before the white traders came. On her feet were moccasins beaded in lightning marks that reminded Yellow Bird of his vision and made him wonder whether she saw, as he did, that world beyond. Surely there was something different about those great, impenetrably dark eyes of hers. Everything about her seemed light and graceful except the odd way she sat—not with her feet to one side, as was proper, but out straight.

Worm drew his right index finger across the left as though stripping feathers. In the sign language it meant "Cheyenne." "She is of your people," he said. "Her name is Black Shawl. She is my son's wife."

"He saved my life, Grandmother." Yellow Bird used the term of respect though she was barely old enough to be his mother.

The woman smiled, opened her mouth to reply, then began to cough, rocking back and forth as though the cough might be lulled like a restless baby.

"She has the coughing sickness of the whites," Worm explained. "It stole past our sentries into our village. Many have it. The medicine water does no good. Some have said my son should take another woman to wife. They brought the one who saved her brother at the Rosebud, but my son said nothing and she left. He wants one wife only. An old woman comes now when we need help."

But it was the old man himself who looked after the lodge most of the time, and he took full charge of Yellow Bird. They were constantly together through the Moon of Popping Trees into the Moon of Strong Cold, when blizzards raged and snow drifted into the tepees. That was a time of year when the whole business of life was to survive from one day to the next. The People never fought at that time of year. Even if enemies stumbled upon one another by accident, they would salute and pass on. The white man might have continued the war, but all the passes were closed by now. This was the only consolation the people had, for supplies were short. What there was of food, blankets, and shelter had to be shared with refugees from Dull Knife's people, for this was the village of Crazy Horse.

Yellow Bird had assumed that much, but it was only after a few days, when Black Shawl felt better and could talk, that she told him this was the great war chief's lodge and that the strange, silent man, who wore none of the battle garb that Yellow Bird knew, was he.

"He goes out looking for help," she told him.

"Who can help such a one?" he asked, wondering what a man like Crazy Horse could lack that other men could give.

"He waits for visions," she replied. "There is a cave he goes to. The cave where he found you."

"Do the visions come there?" he asked, fearing that his expressed curiosity was an impertinence.

"No," she said, not seeming to notice or care. Perhaps she sensed an interest that went beyond simple curiosity. "He sees only darkness. He has only his own strength."

During the rare waking hours that Crazy Horse spent in the tepee he sat smoking a short pipe such as a man who has lost high standing must smoke. He appeared to listen, smiled occasionally, sometimes even laughed, but for himself only added a word here and there. Still, there was a force that seemed to radiate from him as perceptibly as heat from a fire. Yellow Bird regarded him with awe and admiration approaching reverence. But love, such as he had had for his mother, he gave only to the old man whose toothless smile of response was so direct and charming, who seemed so amused by his own name and how he came to own it.

Before he told the story he always fumbled through his old antelope-skin pipe bag fringed with porcupine quills. There he kept the willow bark, the sumac leaves, and the buffalo bone marrow for his pipe. Once he had puffed out the first white cloud, his head would lean forward and his eyes would turn toward the fire's glow. The knotted lean fingers would fix themselves to the long pipestem and he would wait for thoughts to shape themselves into words. Once he was launched, he would carry on as steadily as buffalo fat dripping into a fire.

"When I was a young man," Worm began, "my name was Tashunkewilke, the Man Like a Crazy Horse. I had my son's

name then. I was a hunter and warrior for twenty winters."
And he brought out his scars like treasured old tomahawks to
be viewed and admired. "This scar came from a fight with a
Crow chief, and this . . ." He had many scars, each with a
tale, but never had he suffered a splintered bone or a severed
nerve, a gouged eye or an arrow point in the eardrum, none
of those fearful wounds that kill or maim a warrior. Each of
his wounds was a badge and the starting point for telling a
story. "My brother, High Back Bone, made my son his first
bow. My son was named Curly then. His hair was curly as
yours is, grandson, and light. Have you seen that?"

Yellow Bird had noticed. Any bond that linked him with
Crazy Horse was noted and stored, and he felt that Crazy
Horse had observed this detail as well.

"My son was always a warrior," the old man continued, "but
his first fight was almost his last. He shot one of the enemy
who was hiding behind a thick bush. It was a maiden. She
was like his sister, and he could not take her scalp. For a
winter he went with no war party. Only once did he take a
scalp, and that one he threw to the camp dogs. To take scalps
is against his medicine. It weakens him. Look, I have put down
his deeds in pictures, and those of his brother, Little Hawk.
Little Hawk was a great taker of scalps. White men killed
him in the west." This remembrance did not seem to diminish
the old man's pleasure in the telling, and he laughed as the
pictures brought back fierce pride in exploits recalled. But
it was no exploit in battle that had brought about the sur-
rendering of his name. It was the result of a vision quest.
While still called Curly, Crazy Horse had gone out with his
pony and for three days and nights he had kept the vigil, putting stones under his back to keep from falling asleep.

"When even then no visions came, my son decided to ride home. He stood up to find his pony and it came, but it had changed, and it came bearing a rider from that other world. The rider had long brown hair hanging to his waist. He wore no paint, carried no scalps, but he wore a small stone behind his ear. Arrows and bullets flew toward him, but they dropped at his feet. People grabbed for him as he passed, but he shook them off. A storm raged about him, leaving lightning bolts upon his cheeks and hailstones on his body. When the storm passed, a red-backed hawk flew above him, and it was then that Curly knew the rider's face, as surely as if he had seen it in a white man's trade mirror. Since that time, my son's vision has become his medicine, and he goes to battle without a war bonnet or any strong heart songs."

"Can no bullet or arrow touch him?" Yellow Bird asked.

"Only, it is said, when his hands are held by one of his own people. You have seen the dark scar upon his face." Yellow Bird nodded. "That was from such a time." The fire flared, reddening Worm's face with its glow. "I will tell you. After twenty-four winters my son was still alone. The women called him the Old Lone One, for he loved the wife of another, and she loved him. They ran away together. That was a bad thing to do, and her husband, No Water, followed them. Little Big Man was with my son and the woman when No Water came. When Little Big Man saw a fight beginning, he took hold of my son's arm to stop the trouble, and it was then that No Water fired his pistol. The wound has healed, except for the powder burn, but there has always been bad blood between my son and the people from Red Cloud's agency, and much dishonor. That is why Crazy Horse gave up the long pipe of honor and smokes but a small one now."

"Still, he is chief over all," Yellow Bird insisted.

"Because his vision was greater than his foolishness. It is because of the greatness of his vision that I gave him my name and I took another."

"But why such a name as Worm? You are still a great man."

The old man stared piercingly at him as though to weed out any trace of mockery or condescension for his age. Then, satisfied, he smiled. His mouth opened, closed, took a deep drag on his pipe. A phantom snake of smoke traveled across his face. When it had passed, his eyes were fixed and thoughtful. "I am an old man. My hair has turned white as my life has moved toward the icy north. I am good only to smoke and tell stories to little boys. Now my one good tooth aches and that tells me there will be a fight soon. It aches very much. The bluecoats will come." He stared into the embers as though he saw things there. In the silence, Yellow Bird could hear the soft hiss of buffalo chips sifting down into gray ash. Sparks rose toward the smoke hole.

It was the Moon of Frost in the Tepee, and Worm's tooth ached for the next three days. Then the attack came. The braying of a pack mule kept it from being a surprise, and the deep snow slowed the charge. Crazy Horse had little ammunition left, but he was ready with spears and clubs and the few remaining bullets. For four hours he kept the bluecoats, big and clumsy as brown bears in their winter uniforms, stumbling and sliding on the ice-covered cliffs. The bluecoats would call it treachery thereafter, although if Crazy Horse had been a white general it would have been called strategy. Whatever it was, it worked. The people got away while the braves held the crest. Crazy Horse turned his pony back and forth until dusk, urging them on to keep up their courage. The blizzard masked their retreat, and the bluecoat soldiers were left behind with their wounds and their frostbite.

The people retreated from Box Elder Creek. With the snow and the bluecoats, no one could be left behind. One way or another, everyone had to go all the way. It was exhausting. The braves were already beaten down with fighting and now they moved through the snow like lead-shod runners. Only Crazy Horse seemed free of weariness. He broke trail for them, he moved up and down the line of march, more often leading his pony than riding. Faces came alive at his passing, and people pressed around him with tears in their eyes. He made the fearful less afraid, the weary more vigorous. Each one he touched with a bit of glory.

Once during the trek the bluecoats caught up, pursuing the people across a frozen arroyo. Arrows were lofted back upon the soldiers, but they kept coming. At last Crazy Horse started back with only a bow in his hand, but the people would not have it. He belonged to them all and could take no more risks that day. So it was Big Crow, a Cheyenne who had lost his family at the Dull Knife fight, who stood his ground, a feathered war bonnet trailing behind him and a rifle taken from the Greasy Grass in his hands. The soldiers fired. He fired back. Bullets puffed the snow around him. Though bullets struck him, Big Crow stood erect, firing until the people had vanished into the swirling white flakes, and only then did he give up his life and fall.

They kept moving all that night along the Tongue and beyond. The wind howled, the ponies held their tails between their legs, and at last they came to Hanging Woman Creek, where the bluffs stood high against the north wind. It was a good camp, but this was only the Moon of Dark Red Calves. Winter was far from over and the flight had been hard on them all, hardest upon the old and the sick. Black Shawl could scarcely walk. She coughed day and night and the whites of her eyes were full of swimming flakes of blood.

The weakest ponies had to be eaten. The noisiest puppies, those most likely to give the camp away, were also butchered for food, and one by one the other dogs as well. It wasn't enough. A delegation of old people came to talk to Crazy Horse. They were three times his age, some of them, and yet they pleaded with him in Yellow Bird's presence as though they were children. No ordinary man could stand more. No man should have to. "We can't go on," their spokesman said, and Crazy Horse replied in a voice gentle with his own exhaustion, "But we must go on. We must stay together." Nonetheless, thirteen tepees were struck that night. Crazy Horse with his warriors stopped the deserters from going to the agency. Their weapons were taken, their horses shot for food, and then they were permitted to do what they pleased. Every man in the end must decide for himself, and a chief leads by example and not by power. So they stayed and some of them died, but the tribe was together still.

With the threat of desertion past, Crazy Horse seemed more alone than ever. He was rarely in camp, even at night. As far as Yellow Bird could tell, he ate nothing. Yellow Bird's amazement must have shown in his eyes, for Crazy Horse told him, "You think I act strangely. Do not worry. There are caves up there in the bluffs. There the spirits may help me and there I can make plans for the good of my people. Time is short." It sounded as though he had a presentiment of death. "Since I was a boy, I have known man lives in only a shadow

of the real world. One must dream to find it. I had my vision
of how to lead my people in war long ago. Now I must find
how to put them on the road of peace." So saying, he arose and
departed, and the winter took him back to its silent bosom.

The people watched his coming and going, and they wondered why he never tired, and what he saw. Few could tell,
but one of those who knew, even without asking, was Yellow
Bird. He could tell just by seeing Crazy Horse's returning face
that the real world would not reveal itself, that all Crazy
Horse had was the old stubborn knowledge, that his people
could hope only if they stuck together. That wasn't enough.
What the bluecoat soldiers had not done in their savage wolf
attacks, winter was doing slowly. It was breaking them down.
How could they lose with such a man to lead them? And yet
they were losing, and Yellow Bird sensed the chief knew,
though he never would admit it. If only he could find, in those
dark and icebound caves, a vision as true as the one that had
made him a leader in war. If only Yellow Bird could help. He
had seen that land of which Crazy Horse spoke; he had been
there. Perhaps together? And yet, however strongly he resolved to speak out when Crazy Horse was away, his resolu-
tion foundered when the chief reappeared. He was a child, a
stranger, with the white man's tainted blood in his body.

Though winter's teeth began to dull and there were days
that whispered of spring in the Snow-Blind Moon, a few
lodges were struck and their owners vanished. They headed
for the agencies, and this time they were not to be stopped.
As the trails began to open again, Crazy Horse's mother came
from the Spotted Tail agency. She was fat with Wasichu food,
and she urged her son to untie his pony's tail and return with
her. She brought with her a medicine man who called himself

Long Hair, and who claimed he worked with the spirit of General Custer inside him. He let warriors shoot at him, picking the flattened lead from under his breechclout. But when he tried to doctor Black Shawl, she cried out and was no better. Then the old woman spoke of the agency and the white doctor there, with his powerful medicine.

Crazy Horse gave no answer, though the ice had begun to crack in the river. Lodges had been struck before his very eyes, and Yellow Bird had seen him turn away, saying nothing. Then one day they arose at the same time and went outside. It was not yet dawn. A wet snow dripped from the trees. All else was still, and through the dark and haze on the eastern horizon shone the daybreak star.

Crazy Horse spoke. "The Star of Understanding." Yellow Bird said nothing. He seldom did in the other's presence except when asked a direct question. "I have always wanted a son to teach about the sky and the earth, the ways of the bear and the little brothers, the fox and the beaver. Now I think he will not be born. I had a daughter. She died of the coughing sickness. Now I find you. You are like me, your eyes and your hair. Some say you were with Dull Knife and had no father, but for me you were born in the medicine cave. Why, I ask? What is the use of an orphan in wartime? And then I know. I see your eyes, and I know. You see the visions I cannot see. It is said that if one shares his visions with another, it is to give away power."

"I have told no one," Yellow Bird said, wanting to tell all.

"You should not."

"I would tell you."

"And I would listen," said Crazy Horse.

[66]

So Yellow Bird told of the People and the long road, and the great lodge beyond the clouds, and of the white man who stood on one side of the door and the brown man on the other, and how they beckoned him to enter, both of them together. When he was done, Crazy Horse said, "That is a good vision. My visions were always of war. Now they have passed. Only dreams come." His eyes had a faraway look, as though they were accustomed to studying horizons in bright light. "I dreamed of an eagle flying high above the mountains. He wore beaded moccasins, and there was a knife in his side with blood running down, filling them. I think now I am too old for visions."

"You are not old."

"My daughter died last winter. One hundred of my people died this winter. I am that old. Now," Crazy Horse said, "I am told I must take my wife to the Spotted Tail agency or she will die." He had beaten back each fresh assault, as Yellow Bird knew well. The prairie was trampled. His braves and horses needed new pastures. He had endured the winter, he had held them together. Now the snow water roared gray in the canyons, ice piled on the banks, and the geese arrowed north, and his resolve seemed shaken.

Yet he would not be pushed. When Spotted Tail himself came from the agency, Crazy Horse left camp, leaving Worm to receive the agency chief. Worm's old comrade Hump also came from the agency, with his billhook nose and his fat belly. He brought tobacco to lure the people. Crazy Horse did not speak to him, though to Yellow Bird he said, "When the hearts of the women are on the ground, then the people are broken. I cannot make them go with me to the Powder River country, and yet I cannot leave them behind." After this, old Touch the Clouds led many of the people away to the agency, where they surrendered.

It was now the Month of the Spring Moon. Grass shone through the damp earth and snow clung only to the northern shadows when news came that Red Cloud was on his way to speak for Three Stars Crook, to offer Crazy Horse a reservation on the Powder River if he would bring his Oglala in to Fort Robinson.

"Your warriors have no ammunition," Red Cloud said. "Your ponies are thin. Your wife is like bones in a flour sack. You can fight no more."

"You were once a great warrior," Crazy Horse said.

"Those days are done. It is time to leave the path of war. Untie your ponies' tails."

It was the time for a fighting reply, but Crazy Horse said nothing. He went outside and walked to the crest of a nearby hill. Yellow Bird followed him and was not told to leave. He seemed not even to be noticed, and when Crazy Horse spoke, it was not to him. "Wakan Tanka," he began, "take pity on me. In the name of the People I offer you this pipe. Wherever are the sun, earth, moon, the four winds, there you are always. Save the People, I ask you. They wish to live. Guard them always." He left an offering of tobacco. Then, for the first time, he addressed Yellow Bird. "Now I will untie my pony's tail," he said. And so it was done. The great war was over without a fight.

Except in the heart of Yellow Bird, there was little regret. The camp was struck the next day, and nearly two hundred lodges headed south toward the Red Cloud agency and surrender. Yet they went as though in triumph, painted, feathered, riding in silence once around Fort Robinson. First one, then another, finally all the braves were singing a song of war. But it was a hollow song, and it ended when the bluecoats and the Indian police came out to take away their guns. Now Crazy Horse will fight, thought Yellow Bird. He even hoped for this, though it might mean his life, but Crazy Horse slipped his gun from its scabbard and let it fall to the ground. Later they would take the ponies, too.

Many of the older people and those who were ill settled around the agency, for in those first days they were given good rations of blankets and clothing and food. Worm and Crazy Horse went as far away as they were allowed. That was only three miles, to where the spring grass was thick and the cottonwoods feathered their branches like low clouds of pale green. Yellow Bird went with them. Only death could have torn him from those two. There they waited for news of the promised reservation. Instead, General Three Stars Crook came out with other promises: a late-summer hunt so that the People would have meat for the winter, and after that a trip to Washington for Crazy Horse to see the Great Father. "Why?" Crazy Horse replied. "There is no Great Father between me and the Great Spirit." Yellow Bird knew this was more than simple contempt for the white men, for there were rumors that came from the sit-around Indians that once Crazy Horse was drawn away from his people, he would be sent to a place called the Dry Tortugas from which there was no return.

So spring came, bringing the small game, and with the small game the agency food got worse. In early summer there were stories of how Sitting Bull had gotten away and was living free with his people in Canada. Restless braves began planning for the summer sun dance. They fought mock re-enactments of the battle on the Greasy Grass, and only Crazy Horse riding between them kept blood from flowing.

Then, in the Moon of Cherries Ripening, came word from beyond the Shining Mountains that the pony-breeding people, the Nez Percé, had gone on the warpath against the bluecoats, that they had won many battles and were fighting their way north to join Sitting Bull. At the agency, the soldier chiefs were hiring Sioux braves to go as scouts against the Nez Percé, and some allowed themselves to be bought. They put on the bluecoat uniform and marched away, though Crazy Horse talked out against it and sat silent in his lodge once they had gone.

Yellow Bird knew now that the great warrior had untied his pony's tail forever. He would fight no more, neither white man nor Indian. But Yellow Bird heard, too, that the interpreter, a Kanaka from the Sandwich Islands, who could not speak well and who hated Crazy Horse, had translated Crazy Horse's refusal into a pledge to join the Nez Percé and fight until all the white men were slain. All this Yellow Bird reported to Crazy Horse, adding, "The bluecoats will make trouble. They will lock you up."

"How can I make war?" Crazy Horse replied. "I have no gun. My braves have no guns."

"They say Red Cloud will lock you up if the soldiers don't. They say he hates you, because you divide his people and wish to be head chief over all."

"I want only two things," Crazy Horse replied. "A reservation for my people and strong medicine for Black Shawl. There is a white medicine man coming to see her."

The doctor came the following day. Yellow Bird met him at

the edge of the camp. He had brought his own wife, who wore a black cloth transparent as smoke over her face and rode on her horse in a strange way, as if she had only one leg. The doctor, too, was strange. His black bag was full of colored bottles, and he pressed a black listening trumpet against Black Shawl's back and breast. He smoked no sacred pipe, and called on no gods to help him, but he said that if Black Shawl were to live, she must go to the Spotted Tail agency, which had a doctor with more powerful medicines to fight the coughing sickness.

"That would be good," Crazy Horse said. It would be good for Black Shawl and good for him, for he had been warned, and Yellow Bird knew the warning was true, that Three Stars Crook was planning to send soldiers out to arrest the chief. At Spotted Tail he might be safe with his old friends Touch the Clouds and Little Big Man. They left that afternoon, with Black Shawl wrapped in a red trade blanket and mounted on her spotted pony. Crazy Horse, clad simply as always, did not look like the great chief he was in his deerskin leggings and dark-blue shirt, with only one feather in his hair. A few friends rode with them. Yellow Bird had wanted to go, but Worm was to stay in Crazy Horse's place, and Yellow Bird would have to look after the lodge.

"Remember this," Crazy Horse said before he turned his Appaloosa away. "Never sell the earth upon which the People walk." How could I, Yellow Bird wanted to reply. But the chief was already riding away with the weight of those dark times seeming to rest no more heavily upon him than the air through which he passed.

Though Yellow Bird expected anxious days to pass before there was news of Crazy Horse, things happened quickly. A few hours after the chief's departure, soldiers arrived in the camp to arrest Crazy Horse. They had agency trackers with them, and they set out upon the trail, which was in no way concealed. There was conversation between Yellow Bird and Worm after this. Everything was said with the eyes, confirmed in motion; the packing of what food they had, the closing behind them of the tepee flap. Only one old pony remained to them. They could not ride him fast, but there were Indians along the way who told them of Crazy Horse's passage. They had seen him riding with his friends and two loyal braves. They had seen the soldiers join him, not arresting him but riding along as friends toward Spotted Tail. Outside the agency, the rest of the story was revealed. Crazy Horse had ridden in and been arrested there, not as some said by the soldiers or by the agency, but by a friend, Little Big Man, who for so long had promised to kill the first chief who tried to sell the Black Hills. Now the white men had bought Little Big Man for gold, and they had made him chief of police at Spotted Tail.

From Spotted Tail, the arrested chief was escorted to Fort Robinson. Many of his people followed, among them Worm, Yellow Bird, and Black Shawl. Once there, they set about building the sick woman a shelter with blankets, for the day was late. The nights were already cold, and there was no way of telling how long Crazy Horse would be held. They found out soon enough when Crazy Horse appeared under guard, striding ahead of the bluecoats as though he pulled them along by strings.

"What is that place they go to?" Yellow Bird asked. Though he had seen nothing of white men's buildings before, there was something about this place he did not like. The squareness of it, the dark and joyless slabs of wood, were unlike the gay roundness of the lodges he knew.

"It is a place for prisoners," Worm said. "A cage."

Crazy Horse did not seem to realize this, for he entered without hesitation. The others followed. The door closed on silence. Shadows stretched themselves, and then there was a muffled shout.

"Kill the son of a bitch!"

To Yellow Bird, the words conveyed no meaning. After that, it was shouting without words, and finally the door crashed open and figures were ejected as though from a slide. Two of the figures rose painfully. Another lay there gripping the shaft of a bayonet that protruded from his side as though he feared it might be taken from him. So for a moment all action froze, becoming an agonized tableau in which the only motion was the pouring out of blood, a crimson lake seeping into the dust while Crazy Horse held onto the bayonet as though it were the linchpin that kept his torn body together. He made no outcry, but final defeat showed in the tormented lines of his face.

Then life moved on again. Yellow Bird and Worm ran to the fallen man. A brave named He Dog brought a red trade blanket. An army doctor was sent for and came. Very gently he took the bayonet away, looked at the wound, and shook his head.

"Let his people have him. He can do no harm now," he said, but the officer in charge ordered Crazy Horse carried to the adjutant's office. There the room was square but not barred as the guardhouse had been, and the bare walls were lit by a guttering kerosene lamp. Yellow Bird entered the white man's lodge as apprehensively as though he were stepping into a spring-loaded trap, but Crazy Horse was there, the red blanket wrapped around him. Worm was beside him, looking very old in the orange light, and Touch the Clouds.

Occasional bursts of whispered conversation throughout the dragging hours of the night would piece together what had happened. On seeing the bars inside the guardhouse and men chained by the legs, Crazy Horse had behaved as any cornered creature sure of its strength would have done. He drew his only weapon, a small hunting knife, the blade fashioned of thin sheet steel. He was ready to strike the first hand laid upon him. The hands came unseen from behind, the hands of Little Big Man. Then the guard, William Gentles, his chin heavily bearded, was ordered in. The bayonet rode on his musket without having been locked in place, and so it stayed in the wound. There was one thrust only, into the side of the man who throughout his life had been immune to harm, but that was enough. Crazy Horse in falling gained the door, shoving two guards ahead of him, and then his strength was gone. "Let me go, my friends," he said. "You have hurt me enough."

Outside in the night, chanting voices rose and fell like winter wind in the trees. It was the death chant.

"No. He won't die," Yellow Bird insisted. He could not die, any more than the world could end.

"I am tired of fighting," the wounded man replied. Yellow Bird put his hand on Crazy Horse's forehead. He had never touched him before, but now he kept his palm there as though to smother the pain or to draw it out of him, through his own fingers, into his own body. They spoke little. Crazy Horse's breath bubbled every time he breathed. Toward morning his breath fluttered in his throat and his lower lip drew in between the strong teeth. Blood was mingled there with saliva.

Finally he managed a whisper without any breath behind it. "Father?"

"My son, I am here." Worm leaned toward him, with a harsh whisper in reply.

"Ah, my father. I am badly hurt. Tell the People to look for someone else." He tried to say more. One braid slid from under the blanket to the floor. Touch the Clouds replaced it. The wounded man lay thus for some minutes, scarcely breathing. Then, with a sign as though a ghost passed from him, his mouth gaped. The strange warrior chief of the Oglala was dead.

The old men wept for him, the drops oozing down from crusty eyelids to slowly streak and spread over the stitched wrinkles of their cheeks. Yellow Bird did not cry. For him, Crazy Horse was not dead but gone to that other land to which one day he would find the path.

No one entered the adjutant's office, nor did anyone leave it, yet the news of his death must have been sensed like a change in the wind, for lamentation spread throughout the camp long before the sun rose. At dawn, the doctor returned. He didn't even bend down, but simply checked off something on a pad of paper and departed. A wooden box was found. Two soldiers brought it in, and Crazy Horse, now wrapped in the red blanket, was bundled into it. The soldiers had been instructed to drive home the nails before the corpse was released, which led to a rumor throughout the camp that almost sent the braves upon the agency with flaming arrows. It was said that Crazy Horse had been cut in half. The box seemed too small to hold so great a one as he.

The soldier chief ordered that the body be buried quickly without ceremony lest the Indians in their grief turn to vengeance. To this end, he offered a wagon. Worm would not have it. A travois was the Indian way, and to this the body was lashed. Yellow Bird hitched up the old white-faced bay with the white hind legs. Crazy Horse's mother, who years before had forsaken the harsh ways of freedom for an agency life, joined them on a brown mare. These three alone took the body of the chief for burial. They went first to Pepper Creek, where many Indians still swear Crazy Horse lies buried, but, finding wolf tracks and fearful for the grave, they moved on to another creek called Wounded Knee.

Under a slim horned moon, Yellow Bird dug the grave. The gravelly soil resisted, wanting more competent shoveling, and the moon was nearly down when he finished. He straightened up and flung down the shovel, which quivered upright in the mound like an arrow. It was just a bundle, a bundle wrapped in a red blanket that they were letting down, he thought. And yet with every denial, he knew. He would himself be dead before a man such as this came again among the People. Not in his lifetime would there be such a leader. "Why is he dead?" he asked himself, "and I still here?" How could he carry on? Crazy Horse had been no ordinary man. Wakan Tanka had made him different for a purpose, but there were stronger Gods. His purpose had been a losing one, however glorious. It had been too much for one man to bear unfaltering into old age. How then could he, a boy, his blood tainted by the white man, hope to push on further? How could he hope to show the People the light of a world that Crazy Horse could scarcely see himself?

The grave was filled, the surface swept clear of all traces. No monument was left behind. When Black Shawl died soon after, she was wrapped in deerskin that had been creosoted with smoke, and buried, but Yellow Bird could not be certain that she lay beside her husband. What did it matter where the bodies lay? They were one with the grass. Where their spirits were, there, thought Yellow Bird, it would be good to be.

IV

Land of the Grandmother

If the Great White Father's heart was full of tenderness for
his red children, if he wanted them to live as he said he did,
then why had the Black Hills and the hunting grounds been
taken away? Why had he killed Crazy Horse and driven Sitting Bull to the Land of the Grandmother called Canada?
Why had the People been left nothing but a barren strip
along the Missouri River? The questions were asked over and
over and variously answered among the warriors and in the
councils of the Big Bellies, which Yellow Bird now often at-
tended with Worm. There it was said that the whites wanted
to make Red Cloud the head chief of all the Oglala—Red
Cloud who had grown old, who looked toward the promised
Missouri agency as a soldier's mule looked for its corn. If
they accepted the peaceful way and went to Missouri, they
would have the trade goods, the blankets and the pots, the
iron for arrowheads, and that was about all. How much was
what the whites called peace worth? The alternative was war,
war without ponies and without guns. Not even a bow could
be borrowed in wartime, and the whites were as many as the
blades of grass on the plains. Kill one, kill many, and they
would not be missed. Even if they fought among themselves
and their bodies piled up as fast as driven snowflakes, there
would be more beyond counting. Perhaps Wakan Tanka in-

tended the land for the white man and wished the red man to die. It might be so.

Worm believed it. "I am too old and dry for tears," he said. "I cried for my son. Now I weep no more." But Yellow Bird felt like a bobcat stuck in a cage—and now they were to be moved to a smaller cage. Red Cloud had already gone with his people. The jerky was packed in parfleches for travel, the women had loosened the lodge stakes for rapid striking. Word only had to come from the soldier chief, and the People would head for the Missouri.

The day came in the Moon of Falling Leaves. The morning star still hung in the rainbow-tinted haze of dawning day when the long column led by bluecoats formed and began the trek northeast toward the barren land far from home. Yellow Bird and Worm were near the end of the column. It was during the second day of trekking that the first braves broke away. Yellow Bird thought they were after game, but they were not seen again.

Worm was not surprised. Many had wanted to head north to join Sitting Bull or the Santee who had lived for many years in the Land of the Grandmother. It was the thing to do if one was a warrior, but it was not for the old or those with families.

There was much talk around the campfires that night. The People were many, the soldiers few, and the following day more of Crazy Horse's people broke from the line. It was Yellow Bird's way, the reckless way of freedom, and he was drawn after them as helplessly as iron to a lodestone. "Grandfather," he called back to Worm, who still rode at the end of the column, hunched on his pony. His hair was pure white in the sunlight, his face dark as dried buffalo meat, his great knotted hands resting limply on the nose rope. He looked very

old then, and very tired. Yellow Bird drew his pony to a halt.
He loved Worm more than the dream of the red road and
freedom.

Then Worm was urging his horse, giving it the call to action.
"Hopo! Hopo!" His legs dug into its sides. Yellow Bird rode
to meet him and laid a hand on the nose rope as though to
turn both ponies back. "No," Worm commanded. "I am an
old man, but I am still very strong. Don't worry. Now go."
They were far behind the People, but not so far from the bluecoats, who had left the column and were galloping toward
them. They could not outride their bullets, but they would not
turn back. Better to die, and so they kept riding. Yellow Bird
felt his back stiffen against the coming impact of the first bullet. "It's a good day to die," he told himself. "It's a good day.
It's a good day . . ." The first shot picked up dust ahead of
them and snarled angrily away. Another buzzed like a hornet
and passed overhead. Then a ragged volley alerted the runaway
braves up ahead. A score of them turned back. They were
armed only with bows, but they were enough for the handful of
bluecoats.

They were free. As Yellow Bird paused for a last glimpse
of the People heading east, the air had a richer taste. He could
live on that air alone.

"They are taking the black road, Grandfather. It has no
ending," he said.

"The bluecoats will not forget us," the old man replied.
Then, speaking beyond Yellow Bird, he added a prayer.
"Earth, hide us. Hide our people. Grasses of the earth, hide our
flesh."

The days that followed, one round and perfect day after
another, seemed to confirm for Yellow Bird the belief that

this remnant of the People, Cheyenne and Sioux together, had found the red road at last. Each frosty morning the prairie was covered with melting diamonds, each one a drop of sky, reflecting another world, whispering a promise to come. In the distance were mountains, dark with timber, purple with haze, the snowy peaks gleaming.

"The mountains never change. We grow stiff and old, but the mountains stay the same," Worm said.

"Grandfather, are you glad we came?"

"I am glad," he replied. "I am glad we are together. I haven't traveled this way in many winters. Soon we will be in the country of the Crow people."

"They all scout for the bluecoats."

"Many do."

"And they are cowardly and run away, I have been told."

"Now that they fight for the army. Not when they fought for themselves. All men are that way."

They kept on north through the Powder River country. Geese and green-headed duck flew above them, heading south, and it was their flocks, taken from lakeside cover, that furnished most of the food for the refugees. Here the older men excelled. Their sons had relied on firearms too long and were less skilled with the bow. There was much jest and fun-making around the fires, and pleasure in the old ways come back.

It was on such a hunting excursion that Yellow Bird encountered his first Crow Indians. They were thickset men with bushy heads, and he found them ugly, and their women too; not the sort upon whom he would carelessly turn his back. Fortunately it was a small party on the move and, like the bluecoats, they did not seem ready to risk a few bullets against many arrows.

They moved always north toward winter, toward the sources of the icy blue rivers and the cold lakes of the snow country. Though scouts rode the back trails, there was no sign of bluecoats or of other Indians in pursuit. They had left all behind and seemingly had found a new land fresh from creation. All felt it, and when a girl raised her trill of joy, thin and clear, she was joined by more strident voices. It was a wordless song of freedom, cut short when they came upon a narrow-gauge railroad track. Yellow Bird had never seen an iron road, let alone the fire wagon and the wooden houses that traveled upon it.

"The fire wagon has a great stomach, and the white men feed it wood and water to make it work," Worm told him.

Some of the braves were for catching the train when it tried to pass, but the Big Bellies advised against it. They made the People hurry along toward the border, which they said was near, but some of the braves slipped back after the People had passed. Yellow Bird saw them go to spread the iron road apart so that the fire wagon would fall down. They were across the valley, climbing the facing hill, when it happened. With a shower of sparks and a long and lonely cry, the fire wagon bounded down the slope, and Yellow Bird watched with horror what appeared to be the death of a dragon. The iron beast perished amid a scalding hiss of steam, and presently the braves returned. They had found firewater in the wreckage, and bolts of cloth, which they'd tied to their ponies' tails.

It was a great thing to do, but Yellow Bird knew that it might bring the bluecoats after them. A sense of hurry stole over the People, and they stayed on the trail until after dark. This was lake country, where the water was translucent and full of trout. His pony drank deep, burying his muzzle up to the nostrils: a good sign, for an animal in poor health only touched his lips to water.

The tracks of many unshod horses told them they were nearing their destination. On a bright morning in the Moon of Water Freezing, a valley opened before them, a vast hollow basket, the sides black with firs, the bottom rich in pasture. There were two great white camp circles of Hunkpapa, Oglala, Sans Arc, even a cluster of Nez Percé who had fled the blue-coats only days before. Shouting braves galloped out to greet the arrivals. Their weapon hands were empty. "You are welcome," said their spokesman. "Here the white Grandmother does not lie to the People."

Very few Cheyenne had made it across the border. Because Worm was revered for his wisdom and for his son, he and Yellow Bird were allowed to put up their lodge among the Oglala. The lodge poles, which would have slowed their flight, had been abandoned. New ones had to be cut and stripped and set up, first as a tripod of three key poles. Then lesser poles formed the sacred round upon which the skin of buffalo hides would be stretched. The old seams were spread. They could be patched with rabbit skin, and the inner liner that Worm had painted with his son's great deeds was sound. It would keep out the stormwind. His father's pipe, his bow, all his sacred things, Worm hung at the back in a man's place. Yellow Bird began the first fire, which it would be his task to keep alive throughout the winter to come. The smoke began to lift, sought out the vent, and so it was done.

The next day Yellow Bird explored the great camp, and it was as though his dreams and visions had come to pass in this rich valley where all the People were together, without enemies, without white men. Many of the young women had cast aside the trade goods and wore doeskin again. Their faces were painted in ocher and vermilion. The older women wore necklaces of elks' teeth and seashells. They sat outside all day long making moccasins for the winter to come, their backs braced against the skirts of their tepees. Only with the cool of early evening did they stir up the cooking fires, when the braves were returning from the hunt, shouting their war cries. Then it was the time for talking in the lodges of old wars and hunts to come, of other tribes, and of the mysteries of this world and the next. It was the time for firelight and the flying up of sparks, of song and dance and the dreary chant of a shaman calling on the great forces; time for the brave to slip away to a nearby hillside and sound his lovelorn flute; time for the buffalo gnats to rise in clouds like flung dust; time for the elk to throw his whistling call across the sleeping meadows.

White, wolfish winter would come early in the Land of the Grandmother, but its teeth were dull that year and Yellow Bird was ready for it. With Worm's help he had made snowshoes. Small game was still plentiful, and, once he became expert with the rawhide and wooden frames upon his feet, he could overtake deer and rabbit in the drifts. That first winter was a good one, living snug under the high mountains that moved always with you, white and still under the lowering blue; a good winter for eating and hearing tales of war and spirits and the wandering wolf. He had no regrets about Red Cloud and the new reservation on the Missouri where the old chief and his sit-abouts lived on the white man's dole.

Spring came with the chinook wind, cracking the ice in the rivers. It brought the first Crow raiding parties and a skirmish near the camp in which the cripple called One Who

Never Walks rode out in a basket tied to a travois behind his pony, fought, and died. Afterward they would call him Bull's Heart. In this fight a Crow warrior foolishly broke into camp. Perhaps his pony had run wild. Yellow Bird, firing his first hostile arrow, actually struck the flying figure in the leg, but it was the women who brought him down. With belt axes, skinning knives, and sticks, they set upon him, and Yellow Bird, who went when it was over to retrieve his lucky arrow, found it had been destroyed along with the man. All that remained to tell of a living human was the large, brilliant, and astonished eyes with their long fine lashes. Yellow Bird stood transfixed. He sees, he told himself. Dead, he sees what I long to see.

After the victory over the Crow, a sun dance was called for at Forest Butte. Blue Thunder made the announcement around camp in a voice so loud he had to cover his own ears not to hurt them. The dance was no surprise. It took place every year in the Moon of Making Fat. It was necessary for man to tax himself, for all necessary things came forth from pain: the birth of a child, the splitting of the clouds to make rain. What did surprise Yellow Bird was that Worm declared his intention of taking part, and in the center of the ceaseless flow of dancers the old man stood all day upon a buffalo skull facing the sun. In this way he hoped to call the buffalo up from the south. When the day was done and the red sun burrowed into the mountains, Yellow Bird had to help him home. Worm could scarcely walk. His eyes, sucked by horseflies and bleeding all around the rims, seemed to stare through Yellow Bird as though he were made of glass.

The following day Worm was to smoke with Sitting Bull and the other Big Bellies. Yellow Bird had to lead him to the gathering. There were famous men of peace and war, and in the center of all was Sitting Bull. Yellow Bird had seen him only at a distance before, performing the sun dance or walking barefoot in the dew before the dawn with his young twins, listening to the heart of the earth. Now they were face to face and Yellow Bird saw indeed that he was old, though no part of him had begun to droop. His hooked nose was imperial, his eyes fierce and bloodshot from the sun, his body broad and hard as the trunk of a tree.

"This is Yellow Bird," Worm told them all. "He is my eyes. One day he will be a shaman among the People."

For Yellow Bird it was a great and terrible moment to stand amid such men; to have Sitting Bull take his hands in the cross-armed handshake of respect. But it was a moment soon passed over, for it was time to smoke the sacred pipe. Among these men, seeking enlightenment and a way for their people, the red willow bark was smoked and offered by one and all to the sacred persons dwelling at the four directions. First the bowl was pointed to where the sun rises to revive mother earth with its rays, then to Sovota, the warm god of the southwest, where thunder abides and from where rain comes to turn the earth green. Next was honored Onxsovon, the golden-yellow guardian of the northwest, where the sun leaves the world, and last of all the fearful one, Notomota, the lord of storm, disease, and death, who brooded always beyond the northeastern horizon.

Sitting Bull called on them all in a deep and rumbling voice that had the music of rivers in it. "The Great Spirit has made no lines. The buffalo on both sides of the white stone heaps taste the same. Why do the Americans keep us from feeding our people? Why may we not hunt the buffalo beyond the stone heaps? If we may not, O spirits, make the buffalo come to us. Make them come, or the People will starve." He shook his head like an old horse bothered by flies. None of them wanted anything to do with the Americans. They had stolen the Indians' country. At least the Queen's commissioners spoke true. They left the People alone so long as they did not cross the line to where the Americans lived. Sitting Bull told of his trip to Fort Walsh. With the redcoats of the Mounted Police all around, he had been afraid, but they had not touched him. Even when he would not talk to Star Terry, who wanted him back at the agency, they had protected him. Why did the Americans want him back? They had killed his friends. Did they wish to kill him, too? "You have stolen the Indians' country," he told them. "Keep it. Better to go to a hilltop for water than to an American for truth or help." They would stay and pray for the buffalo to come, he had said then, and he had not changed now. The others signaled agreement. There was no other way.

Throughout the summer they prayed and waited and watched. Few buffalo appeared and the smaller game was vanishing. Some braves crossed over the border beyond the stone piles. Since this made trouble with the redcoats, Sitting Bull had the braves hung naked with their toes barely touching the ground. They hung there all day, blind with pain, their bodies black with hungry mosquitoes. Only at night were they cut down.

Autumn came early. The Moon of Ripened Cherries brought the pink bloom of the rattlesnake root and the hard wind that peeled off the leaves. A great prairie fire blown by that ceaseless wind destroyed much of the forage for the pony herd, and Yellow Bird knew that the winter in store was meant to punish them. But why? What had they done now? Why were the rabbits gone from the fields, and the deer from the hillsides? Why had the ducks gone south so early? Why had the sun stolen the old man's eyes? Worm sat most days bunched up before the tepee like a blind bat, hoping the sun would soak the stiffness out of his joints. It was hard for Yellow Bird to imagine being that old. Sixty, seventy winters. He felt he must have been born without an old man inside him. What did Worm see with those sun-struck eyes? They looked older than one man's living, seeming to stare through everything to the horizon. Did he glimpse that world beyond and see the Gods? A medicine man named Creeping, who had cured snow blindness, came and blew the first snow into Worm's face, but the old man only smiled at his efforts. He continued to gaze at the horizon, and he said, "I would not want to see any farther than I see now."

"Come inside, Grandfather," Yellow Bird urged him. "The sun has gone down."

"Yes, it is cool." Worm winced with the sharpness of his joints as he stood up. Yellow Bird took his hand and he followed with a submissive step, his heels striking the ground with a jolt. He sat quietly before the lodge fire, rocking slowly while Yellow Bird prepared the meal. He had learned much about fires and cooking. They ate without conversation, revering what food they still had. Then, when the fire glowed low, throwing soft shadows on the lodge walls, the old man would cough. This was a way of bringing attention to himself, for he liked to tell of the old hunts and of the beauty and strangeness of the earth. He did so with gaiety and good cheer, for he was a weary old man only in his muscles and bones. His spirit remained indomitable.

"Let me tell you how Sitting Bull's uncle, Four Horns, became head chief," he began. "It is a good way to tell a great man. In those days the Hunkpapa had four chiefs. Besides Four Horns, there was Loud-Voiced Hawk, Running Antelope, and Red Horn, and when the People decided one alone should be chief over all and none could say who it should be, the Big Bellies decided on a test. Each chief's favorite wife was stolen away, and each chief was told by a gossip the name of the seducer. Three of the chiefs rode off, looking for revenge, but Four Horns kept his temper and put the People first in his thoughts. He did not leave them while the other three made fools of themselves, and so it was that he became chief over all."

"I wonder, did Four Horns love his wife?" Yellow Bird asked.

"He loved her. It would be a foolish story if he did not," Worm replied. "Shall I tie another story to that one?"

"Your stories are good, Grandfather, but I must hunt before the sun awakens."

"A boy needs sleep. I will awaken you when it is time."

Yellow Bird built up the fire. When he lay down, Worm was already asleep. His little groans as he shifted his weight made the boy smile. He fell asleep so suddenly at times that Yellow Bird would think he had died, but he woke as easily and often, his night being a shallow one of short naps in which his thoughts galloped over the great plains through endless grass high as his pony's chest, to where the herds of buffalo blackened the horizon.

That year and again the next year the snows came early and did not melt. The lakes froze, and Yellow Bird could chop away with a good tomahawk for half a morning, leaving its blade dull as a stone, before cutting through to water. He hunted or fished every day. The weather made no difference and the process did not break him down. Instead, he felt a new trimness about his body. He was growing taller, stronger. Most hunts were alike, beginning in the darkness, looking all day for a rabbit, losing him as often as not but sometimes getting in a fatal shot or chasing the creature into a drift where he might be taken. It was not until the Snow-Blind Moon, when he could not move from the lodge without snowshoes, that the strange hunt took place.

Worm awakened him, as he did each morning, before the sun showed itself. He was like a worried mother, concerned that Yellow Bird take every precaution against the cold, the snow, wandering Crow warriors, the spirits of ice and snow.

"Do not forget extra thongs for the snowshoes," he cautioned.

"I have them, Grandfather."

"Take your medicine bundle. It has the power of God."

"I have everything, Grandfather. You are the forgetful one. One man does not always tell another what to do."

"You are right, grandson. I haven't died, but already I have begun to haunt." He was smiling. "But remember what I have said."

"I will," Yellow Bird replied, raising the tepee flap. Outside, it was black night still and he plunged into it. A pale shaven moon gave no real light. Wind whispered over the snow, which was as dry as dust. It cut through his blanket like a blade of ice and made him shiver. With the dawn he would trot himself warm, and he must be glad of the snow, which was not his enemy as it was the enemy of those creatures which he hunted.

By midday he had spent one arrow, having loosed it in

wobbly flight after a rabbit. By then the wind had shifted and turned moist. He could feel it in the scar left from the Dull Knife fight. The sky had become a dull sheet of iron that he knew would, before dusk, begin to cast down snow. He should have turned back, but he was reluctant to do so empty-handed, and the sight of a distant elk made up his mind. He pressed on even as the first ragged flakes announced the rolling storm. With three arrows between his teeth for rapid firing, Yellow Bird went to where the elk had stood. The snow fell in screens, opening and closing. He saw no sign of the elk, which must have been on its way to the shelter of a canyon, as he should be. Moving toward lower ground, he thought he saw it again, blurred and uncertain. He followed, lost it, and then came face to face with a grizzly bear that rose suddenly from behind a fallen tree, its forearms pressed against its body. Its paws hung in surprise as though it were just rising from prayer.

Yellow Bird had weapons to wound but never to kill such a beast. He backed off respectfully as the bear seemed to lean toward him. "Brother bear, I will not hunt you if you will not hunt me." Never taking his eyes away, he kept on backing. The bear receded as a stone settles through water, lost, seen again, vanished finally. Yellow Bird was about to turn and run when his backward-feeling foot found nothing but a steep incline and he tumbled through thick pine needles to the sheltered base of a tree. Here was a natural lodge with fuel enough for a small fire. If the bear did not come, he resolved to stay while the storm lasted.

It took two nights and a day for the storm to blow itself out. He was cold but not frostbitten, and his parfleche contained enough dried venison to keep his stomach from cramping. Scratching for fuel beneath the snow, he discovered during the long day the body of a foal, perfectly frozen and preserved. If he could wait out the storm, he would take it home. They would have a splendid feast then. He would dig out a hole, cover it with hot stones and embers for hours. The meat would be so tender even Worm could chew it with his gums.

The wind died at dusk. A slow, heavy-flaked snow still fell throughout most of the night. When it stopped just before dawn, there was a stillness over all, a stillness in which he heard the howling of a wolf or a coyote; he couldn't be sure which, the cry was so strange. Both creatures were his brothers. They used up dead things that would poison the air, and in that howling now he heard, not words, but a message that seemed plainer than words. It told him to go home, to hurry.

The landscape had changed a good deal, but he knew from the wind dugouts which were the northwestern slopes. With the foal stiff as a log across his shoulder, Yellow Bird jogged forward. He trotted mindlessly until he confronted a knife slash of a gorge cut by a frozen river, filled with great buffeting hunks of piled-up ice. He had to take off the snowshoes to get across. Jogging again, his leggings hammered against his pumping legs like sheet metal.

Yellow Bird was exhausted when he finally tore open the lodge flap, but he didn't feel as bad as the old man looked. His face was a shaman's wooden mask. The mouth lolled open, lopsided. The tendons of his throat stood forth. Yet there came the familiar concerned voice. "Grandson, I was worried."

Yellow Bird flung down his burden. He knelt by the old man. "Grandfather, are you sick?"

"I'm tired," came the distant reply.

"Do you want water?" Yellow Bird offered him water from

a horn drinking cup, but the liquid spilled down his chin. Within an hour the meat was thawed out. Yellow Bird made a broth with some of it, but the twisted mouth said no to food. Overcome by his own hunger, Yellow Bird roasted a piece of flesh over the fire. The juices ran out, making the flames spurt up. He couldn't wait until the meat turned crinkly brown, but ate it red, with ice chips toward the center. Only then was he able to get food into Worm, whose wasted throat moved laboriously as he took a cup of broth.

In the morning the old man ate again. He seemed better. Only his talk was worrisome. "Your grandfathers were honorable men," he said. "Generation after generation." He seemed to think Yellow Bird was of his own blood. "You may be worthy to stand with them one day. But I see the dark road ahead. It must be walked if the People are to live. You may be the one to lead them."

"I can't," Yellow Bird told him. It was that chill hour of a winter night which congeals the blood of beasts and men. "If Sitting Bull can do nothing, what can I do?"

"You can try. You can pray as your heart commands."

"Grandfather, you must show me the way."

"My path is short, grandson. It leads to Wounded Knee. Grandson, will you take my bones to lie with my son at Wounded Knee?"

"You aren't dying, Grandfather. The meat will give you strength."

The old lips moved slowly, preparing a statement. "Take courage, grandson," they said. "The earth is all that lasts. Beyond, the water is sweet and the grass is green and the white man can never go." After that he lay smiling, eyes open upon another kind of dream. Yellow Bird clung to him, a weary child grown old, while Worm turned cold in his arms.

In the morning Yellow Bird wrapped the old man in his red blanket. The ground was frozen beyond digging, but the snow was deep enough to hold the tall cottonwood poles for a funeral scaffold. Upon this Worm was laid to rest with his shield and his spear and his old war bonnet with most of the feathers gone. When this was done, Yellow Bird painted his face black with soot in sign of mourning. There was a time, he knew, to be borne in arms, and a time to walk with one's family. There was also a time to walk alone and to become a man, a time for hunting, and a time for war, a time for a family and a time to die, and he felt without doubt that he had come to the loneliest of these.

He hunted alone and kept the lodge alone, and during that time, without the old man to keep, he had a luxury of days to think and feel. It was in such fertile soil that real hatred began to flower. He had hated and feared his father, all white men, in an abstract way before. His mother's death and Crazy Horse's had been bad things, hurts that were too big to handle, but only now was he consumed with placing blame. If it were not for the white man, Worm would not have died in this frozen, forsaken land. If it were not for them, his mother and Crazy Horse would be alive. Let the white man say the only good Indian was a dead one, but he would not believe that a good white man had yet been born. His eyes, blue with Custer's blue, were cold and opaque as the whipped snow, and remorseless as those of a stalking wolf.

V

Buffalo Bones and London Town

Thunder and the whirlwind were the guardians of the sacred arrows. They were the bringers of spring, driving away Hoimaha, the Winter Man, the bringer of the cold snow death. After the silence of the snow came the whisper of water, water everywhere, growing to a rumble. But the winter of 1880 was not something Yellow Bird could easily forget. Worm was not the only one who had died. Starvation, the cold, and the blizzards had claimed many two- and four-legged ones. They had broken the spirits of others among the People: Big Bellies such as Gall and Crow King who, as soon as the paths were clear, headed south for the Great Sioux Reservation across the border. They went, and no one spoke out against them or tried to stop them.

What had been a great village of one thousand lodges dwindled until by summer there were less than one hundred. Then, when it was nearly time once again for the sun dance, Sitting Bull spoke to his people. "There are no buffalo here. The Grandmother whose land this is will not help us. The Americans arm the Crow and the Bannock to murder our young men when they try to hunt. They, who have taught us how to lie, say they want us back. Why, I ask? So that my body may be food for their dogs? I do not know, but here we are sure to die. So I will tell Le Gare we will go back. We agree, as the buffalo when struck with the hunter's bullets. What can he do then but lie down and die?"

No voice spoke against this. Yellow Bird had lost his early love of the Grandmother's land. The red road was not there. One pony remained to him. He packed his parfleche with robes and his best moccasins, and he carried the tack-studded carbine that had been with Crazy Horse at the Greasy Grass. Beyond these few things he had to choose between the buffalo skins that made up the lodge or the remains of Worm. There was no real choice. The old man had asked to lie with his son, so Yellow Bird cut out one skin from the lodge upon which he had painted his vision of the red road. This he bound around the red-robed, bird-pecked ruin that had been his guardian and waited for Sitting Bull to raise his hand as a sign of departure. Forty lodges, thirty rickety wagons, half of the People mounted, half on foot, they waited reluctant, fearful, saw the moon move down into the trees, the sky brighten in the east. Then with the daylight the French trapper Le Gare came to give them safe conduct to Fort Buford. The trapper and Sitting Bull shook hands, with the chief offering but two fingers in greeting, as he would not offer a full hand of friendship to any white man.

Sitting Bull raised his lance. There was a moment's pause, a kind of shock, as though somewhere a great gong had sounded and they were waiting for the vibrations to be absorbed into the air. The cracking of a whip broke the spell. A pony neighed. Wheels creaked. Head down, Yellow Bird led his pony by a nose rope. Two travois poles dragged behind, leaving a shallow track in the mud. It would rain before nightfall and the mud would grow deep toward the end of the column.

Yellow Bird had no intention of trekking into captivity. He was bound for Wounded Knee, and he needed no companion. The time for letting another lead the way was over. He had the gun and a wooden hoop to which tiny pouches of medicine were tied. His wo-ta-we and his wits would protect him. On the second day, as he sat alone before a small fire, feeling not quite of this world or of the next, neither quite hearing nor entirely deaf to the night sounds, they nearly failed him. A Crow brave, his tomahawk cocked back ready to strike, was into the firelight before Yellow Bird was aware of him. He might have died there, unremembered, leaving his bones to mingle with those of the old man. In thinking about it afterward, he was astonished that he had not frozen stiff like a cornered rabbit. Instead—and he could recall no conscious decision to do so—he snatched up a flaming stick from the fire and dashed into the darkness. Ten, fifteen running steps with his pursuer right behind brought him to the edge of a cliff. His body remembered if his mind did not. As his left arm shot out to grab the trunk of a small tree, he flung the torch straight ahead. It flew out, turned, and plunged down. The Crow went after it. Without a pause, without a cry, he pursued the light into empty air. Yellow Bird listened for the sound of impact. "It's the wind," he told himself. "I would have heard it except for the wind." When he returned to his campfire he extinguished the last embers and lay that night in the dark wondering whether he had been attacked by flesh and blood or by a phantom.

In the morning the river below revealed no secrets and Yellow Bird went on his way, lighting no more fires until the landscape began to look familiar. I know this place, he said one morning. I've camped here before. From then on he stopped here and there with smiling eyes to recognize some familiar aspect of the land. This was home, the Black Hills, his land, although he had not owned a shovelful of it. He had never considered the possibility of possessing that which he believed to be his divine mother, and he could not abide the thought that others, white men, should claim ownership; that they should come with saw and ax and wire; that they should dig into its heart with shovels, seeking gold. His life, whatever it was worth, with whatever strength he had, was set against this happening.

By a roundabout course, avoiding the homesteads that he saw, Yellow Bird approached Wounded Knee. Almost four years had passed since he had visited the place with Worm. He could almost hear the digestive noises of the old man's stomach doing the work his teeth could not, the old man's smell of him. This vivid recollection brought no pain. It was like an arrowhead, lodged and guarded round about by scar tissue, a treasure now. Besides, he felt sure that something of Worm and Crazy Horse stayed with him always, walked by his side by day, guarded him at night. How else could he have escaped the Crow warrior? Without their guidance, surely he would not have found such desperate cleverness. He would have died there, unmoving and undefended.

There was no use seeking out the grave of Crazy Horse. Even if they had placed a marker, it would have been swept away by the rains. So he buried Worm alone by night where no one would find or disturb his bones. He left no monument, for he felt the spot was empty. He could no more bury Worm's spirit than he could plant a puff of breath in a storm cloud.

That was a summer of warm days under the endless blue and cold nights with an icy wind at dusk. Yellow Bird lived out those days alone with only a wickiup of branches and blankets for a home. Wandering the ravines and cutbacks under the dark pine and shivering aspen, he made up songs to the breathing trees, and to the songbirds. He praised the buffalo and the grizzly who had spared his life, and always he shunned the white man. He spoke to few Indians, but those few told him how Sitting Bull had been roughly received by the Indian police who envied his power, how his horses and weapons had been taken, how, despite promises of pardon, he had been put in a cage at Fort Randall and his children kidnapped to white schools far away. Those of his people who resisted were given no rations. None of this came as a surprise to Yellow Bird. He was astonished only that they had not been killed.

Of all the things Yellow Bird discovered about surviving alone in the Black Hills, the most exciting concerned the thunder. Always he had known that when the thunderbirds visited the dark peaks, they brought lightning, and always the boiling storms had filled him with a sense of that other world of strange and holy things but faintly understood. Now the storms did not simply bellow and laugh at the world; they spoke directly to him. Yellow Bird had been terrified at first, and when the intensified odor of leaves and grasses told of a coming storm, he had been filled with apprehension. Like an old woman, he had wanted to screech and shake a blanket, or to fire off his gun at the clouds that devoured the blue. He had longed for a cave where he might hide as the old wind died and shifted around. He wanted the autumn frost to come and put an end to the storms' commands and prophecies.

In time his fears gave way to horrid excitement and finally to ecstatic joy that rose with the gale. An unseen charge of ponies high on the wind trampled down the thunderheads. Great armies of his ancestors were pounding home. Grasses bent down in fear before the flaming hoofs, and he heard them call his name, not always in words, but with a meaning that glowed inside him. "Louder, speak louder!" he shouted into the tumult, knowing that no sound could be louder. The thunder roared back. The wind lashed so that he had to hold on, his fingers gripping the storm-split rock, his breath coming and going harshly. Yellow Bird scarcely felt the rain that rushed down suddenly, wetting him to the skin, plastering down his hair. Water ran out of his eyes and ears and down his neck. He barely felt it, but laughed and struck his fists on the ground, raising his drowned voice in howls of pure elation: "You are not all dead!" There were bright days yet to come if he could but beat his wings against the blast, for, beyond the hail and the lightning, warm sunshine sent down its rays into plains rich in buffalo.

Yellow Bird lay with his face on pine needles. They did not prick his cheek. The rain did not chill him. Nothing mattered, for he felt he was coming into his manhood, his life's purpose, the unfurling of a rainbow. With the clearing skies, birds sang overhead, crowds of them, rivers of birds in flight. They sang inside him. Crazy Horse, Monahseetah, all would return.

Throughout the summer Yellow Bird listened to the thunder. The first mutterings of a rising storm became for him the announcement of an arriving friend. Autumn was a time of regret, of falling leaves and long, lonely nights. One day, when he encountered a hunting party of braves who had lived with Sitting Bull in Canada, he went with them.

"We heard that you were dead," said one named Elk's Belly.

"I was," he replied. "I am alive again."

Elk's Belly looked at him steadily, without comment. Such things happened and were accepted, as was the large medicine bundle that Yellow Bird had collected after listening to the thunder's talk: the feathers of many birds, thonged and beaded together, a deer-bone whistle, and a pouch full of many herbs. Of these things they took note but did not press him, treating him as older than his years. Of the spirit world he said little; of the world of the white man and the Indian he learned much. Sitting Bull had been released, but if the whites thought he had been taught a lesson, they were wrong, for he still made strong heart talk against new treaties that would break up the reservation. Though he was not head chief according to the white man's paper, the People heard him first. Even the whites in Washington seemed to listen, and when the Northern Pacific Railroad drove its last spike in Bismarck, North Dakota, Sitting Bull was invited to speak.

Elk's Belly, who spoke the white man's language, had gone along as interpreter. He had coached Sitting Bull in pretty words of greeting.

"He spoke our language," Elk's Belly recalled. "He spoke long. He told the white people how he hated them, how they were liars and thieves that had taken our land. He spoke the truth. He called them bad things, and they clapped their hands together like this. When he finished, he bowed to them as white men do, and they stood and cheered. Then a bluecoat came to repeat what Sitting Bull had said in their language, but it came out all wrong. He said Sitting Bull had spoken of the good and wise White Father in Washington, of the Indian's love for his white brother, and of his wish to be like him. It was very strange."

"The white man is our enemy," Yellow Bird said. "I would never travel in his land."

"Many braves have gone there and returned, as I have done," replied Elk's Belly.

"If one wishes to become a Wasichu, it is the place to go."

"You do not need to love the white man. Grandson, there is a wise saying among the whites. Know your enemy. Think on that, Yellow Bird."

With the first snows, the hunting party gravitated toward the reservation. Part of Yellow Bird yearned for the solitude that he could trust, but the thunder people had gone south. He did not love winter man who bit with icicle teeth, never spoke, and helped no one. Reluctantly he moved his wickiup onto reservation ground near Standing Rock. With none to support besides himself, he refused agency food—the stringy meat of the longhorn and the salty yellow pork often so moldy dogs would not touch it. He had no taste for the dark and gummy tobacco. Such things turned the People into less than white men.

Though Yellow Bird made no effort to mix with people, he was not ignored. Children, even boys his age, seemed reserved in his presence. He sensed they were intimidated by his strangeness and by his large medicine bundle, which included his own charms as well as those inherited from Worm. Occasionally older men came to him with coughs and minor wounds and dreams, and he did what he could to heal or interpret. He remembered what Worm had told him and what he himself had observed from the doctoring of Black Shawl, and of Worm in his last blindness.

So another winter passed, and when the geese were overhead like flights of arrows, driving winter man back into his black cave, and the bow of a spring moon was looked for in the sky, Yellow Bird was visited by Sitting Bull.

The Hunkpapa chief came quietly and without ceremony. Among the white men, Red Cloud had become like an autumn apple, red only on the outside but white beneath his skin. The whites with their big villages and their presents had ruined him, but Sitting Bull seemed unchanged. He told Yellow Bird of his great friendship for Worm and how much he had heard from him about Yellow Bird. He had learned from others as well of the boy's growing powers.

"I have no powers," Yellow Bird assured him. "I hear the thunder sometimes. It tells me of winters past and of times to come."

"Does the thunder speak of the buffalo?" Sitting Bull asked him.

"Yes," he replied, though usually it spoke to him of other things he did not name.

"There will be a dance," Sitting Bull told him, "to call the buffalo. If the buffalo do not come, the People must starve or all of them become like the white man. You will dance."

Yellow Bird wished only to be left alone, but it is not often that a boy, a boy without one eagle feather, is commanded by such a one. He nodded.

Before the buffalo dance could begin, there was the cleansing ceremony of the sweat lodge. There, in what stood for the womb of mother earth, came new life and new understanding. As the least important of those to enter the sweat lodge, Yellow Bird went first. Sitting Bull came last. All sat cross-legged. Each offered a pinch of tobacco to the sky and to the four sacred corners: "O great spirit, accept my offerings and make me understand." Sitting Bull led the chant. Then the coals arrived, glowing like the eyes of wolves in the dark, and were heaped upon the piled sweet grass. Yellow Bird rubbed in the sacred smoke, though his eyes teared. Finally came the hot stones, glowing radiant and angry, and after them the water. Poured over the stones, water exploded loud as a rifle shot. Then followed a hiss as of giant snakes, filling the enclosure with stifling steam. Near the roof, the heat was killing. Yellow Bird bent low. There was a bitter taste of sage in his mouth, and if any one of them had given up and burst through to the sunlight, to the cool and breathable air, he would have followed. No one moved.

Three times the glowing stones were replaced and three more times the water was brought in, until he thought the flesh would boil from his bones. Four times all endured in silence and then, red as though painted for war, they staggered out, legs rubbery, to plunge into a nearby stream. Yellow Bird floated there, a boneless spirit of the departed, human only in his pride. He had endured. He was purified and ready for the dance.

The bluecoats had forbidden the sun dance. They might feel the same about a buffalo dance, about anything that excited the old ways, so no permission was asked and the hang-around chiefs were not told. Swiftly the sacred lodge was erected in the center of the dance circle and the inner walls were painted with bison and mounted huntsmen. On the eve of the dance, thunder beings rumbled their approval. They had not spoken before in that year, but still something in Yellow Bird held back, made him move slowly as he pulled on the sacred clothing, all of it rawhide and buckskin decorated with shells.

Nothing was made of glass or wool from the agency store. This was the end of something. His solitude? He might put aside these garments, but he would not be the same again. Once he was dressed, the ancient shaman, Ice, painted him with the red-ocher paint, and added the four-rayed star of daybreak upon his face, and the horned moon upon his shoulders. Finally Yellow Bird took in his hand a flowering stick. It represented the sacred tree that must bloom above the People before the old ways and the good road could be found again.

Already the braves had begun. Disguised as buffalo, they pawed the ground, twisted heads in air to the heavy beat of drums, locked shoulders, exchanged blows with their horns. Then Yellow Bird and Sitting Bull and all the shamans among them began to dance, their heavy stabbing steps lifting the dust, moving them in the slow and sacred circle. Drums boomed in the shimmering heat, a thousand bells tinkled. The earth itself seemed to rock, to shift and whirl.

> *A nation is coming, a nation is coming,*
> *The hawk brings the news.*
> *Over the earth they are coming,*
> *Buffalo, buffalo,*
> *The birds say so.*

These words sang in Yellow Bird's head, over and over, and he was scarcely aware that they flew from his lips. There was magic in them, power beyond his power, and he surrendered to the frenzy that rose within him.

> *Under the sun they are coming.*
> *The crow sees them, the crow sees them,*
> *A buffalo nation is coming.*

He saw the black herds thundering in their thousands, saw the clouds of arching birds, saw them all spinning away together as he fell.

Yellow Bird awoke later in the sacred lodge. Outside, the People rejoiced at his vision. Braves paraded, while at his feet, in the sacred circle of smoothed earth that was the world in miniature, he saw tiny hoofprints as though buffalo ghosts had danced there, too.

The next day scouts rode out to find the promised herds, while those who stayed cut up frying pans and iron hoops into the arrowheads they would need for the great hunt to come. None doubted, and there was no great surprise when the shout carried through the village: "Many buffalo I have heard. The birds show them."

Women trilled the news. The camp broke out in song and games as the scouts told of seeing the birds from a distant hill. Then it was the serious business of the hunt, with the honored ones shooting for the old, the crippled, and the blind. Yellow Bird, though his marksmanship was scarcely tried, was one of these, for he was credited in part with conjuring the herd, a vast one if the scouts could be believed, a herd such as had not been seen in years. A chief of the hunt was quickly elected and it was Sitting Bull, of course. He sent out the older hunters in a screen to hold back the youths, eager for a name and impetuous, who were apt to stampede the herd.

One thousand braves rode out toward the Grand and Moreau rivers basin where the sacred hills lay like slumbering black bears upon the rim of the world. The sun rose, a fiery eye to gaze upon their preparations. When the last scouting party returned, its leader touched his two spread hands at the thumbs, then moved them from his right shoulder to his left to signify one hundred. He went on to make the sign again, one hundred hundred, and again. Impossible. "Many, very many," he insisted, as it was before the white man came with his long-range guns; before a good skin bought a jug of whiskey, before sportsmen fired into the herds from halted trains. "See, their breath clouds." In the cool of summer dawning, mist rose above the herds as should only be expected in winter. Then by some miracle, the will of the Gods, perhaps, or because of a mirage as the white man put it, buffalo appeared grazing on the sky. They were enlarged: giant buffalo, moving steadily above the horizon.

Rifle or bow in the right hand, jaw rope in the left, stripped to breechclout and moccasins, Yellow Bird and the others rode. It was as though they went to battle from behind the sheltering hills, whooping through the dust, curving in, one behind the other in two great arcs until part of the herd started to mill. Then the killing began. Huge dark bodies staggered and went down and ponies tripped over the fallen buffalo. Hunters ran on foot, clung to the thick wool of their prey, and sometimes went under. Round and round the killing circle turned, growing smaller until the plain was strewn with the dead.

Yellow Bird found that he could use his bow calmly. The pull and release of the bowstring seemed a physical part of him, and he fired down on the pitching humps until his arrows were almost spent. Then he sat his pony, facing one last bull, which was streaming blood from many arrows. He fired another into its side, and the bull pawed the ground, advancing with a stumbling trot. He fired again. The bull hooked a horn at empty air, swayed, bellowed, its black lips throwing blossoms of blood. Then it stood silent, spinning orange spittle, refusing death until its knees buckled and it fell over on its side. Life fought in retreat, but finally the bull bared grinning teeth and lay still. Yellow Bird dismounted. He swayed as the bull had swayed. All around him braves sat their ponies.

The great hunt was over. In the silence, louder somehow than the subterranean thunder of hoofs, Yellow Bird heard the trilling of the women as they ran out for the butchering. Nothing was wasted. The flesh would be devoured down to the hide and hoofs. The backbone and ribs would become toboggans, sewing needles, ornaments. Much was eaten on the spot. Especially relished by Yellow Bird and the other hunters was a square of intestine salted with a droplet of bile.

It had been a fine hunt. The coming winter had lost its teeth. They would eat. Then why was Yellow Bird dissatisfied? Was there something wrong with the old men coming out to reclaim the arrows, to salvage the tips if the arrows were broken? Was not all as it should be? By evening, long lines of laden ponies, travois piled with fresh-packed flesh, were heading back to camp. Pots were already boiling over there, filled with livers, sweetbreads, tongues. Women found the finest bits for the hunters, for the heroes who gorged and told stories, smoking the pipes, touching them to the ground four times in pledge that what they told was truth. Surely there was nothing wrong in that, or in the dressing of the skins, the curing, the endless scraping and painting on of symbols, figures, dreams of brave men's deeds. All that was as it should be.

In the dark, songs were hastily composed and sung for the hunters who had saved their friend from being trampled, and for the marksman who had placed the first arrow, and the last. When all else was properly done, the finest robe, tanned, painted, worked with beads and quills, was taken to the hill where the herd had first appeared and left there in gratitude to brother buffalo who made it possible for the People to live.

All this was well and properly done, and yet that sense of unease nagged at Yellow Bird and found no resting place. In the autumn, when the buffalo would have their finest coats, only then was another hunt proposed. The scouts rode out in the four directions. For days they came and went, examining old trails, old buffalo chips and wallows. The blue grama grass stood high and empty. They spoke with other wandering hunters. The Crow who were their enemies had no fresh meat in their camps. Some who knew the tongue spoke to the white men who were out with their wagons. The wagons were empty of hides. There were only bones now; only white bones bleaching in an empty prairie.

The buffalo had been without ending. They had vanished before and returned. Yet this time Yellow Bird knew the great herds would not reappear. He knew this with that inexplicable knowledge which draws the goose south in winter, the moth from its cocoon. The buffalo were gone as finally as if Winio, the Wondrous One, had come again and driven them all back into his magic sack. With them had gone the old ways. The road of his people was an ancient and good one, which they had traveled since the world's beginning. Now the road of the buffalo hunter was gone. The corn road was hard. The white men said it was the only way they would live, by planting and reaping, but Yellow Bird knew how often the rain was all wind and the wind all dust. He listened long to the sad and murmurous voice of the wind, and he knew the corn road was not for his people. Their world was a thing of the past and their way was lost.

His heart was bad against the white man, and against Sitting Bull, who had taken many of the best braves and gone east with Buffalo Bill. They would dance before the white man and come back wearing the white man's clothes. They had deserted the People when they were lost, when the brave in his first power could find no eagle feathers to put in his hair. Even the sacred birds were dying of despair. There was nothing now to be courageous about, either in war or on the hunt. The only courage was in keeping down the salt pork and bacon that made Yellow Bird's tongue swell. Even worse was the meat of the wohaw, the lean, stringy spotted buffalo with the long horns which the agency men drove up from the south. They filled them with water at the last to make them seem fat and drove them twice around the hill to make them seem like a bigger herd. They were always shouting "Wo" and "Haw" at the staggering beasts. Once a steer was assigned to him, Yellow Bird would drive it away, as the others did, to the plains, where with his bow and arrow he would slaughter it in the old way of the buffalo. There was no pleasure in doing so, for the creature cared not for life but stood stupidly while the arrows entered, lowing for a land that was lost. It was like putting arrows into his own body.

As much as possible, Yellow Bird kept away from the agency. He hunted small game with a bow and lived in the tattered, wind-whistling remains of a buffalo-skin tepee. Others lived in the white man's canvas. In all things it was hard now to escape the white man's ways. A brave no longer dared cut the nose from his adulterous wife, for fear of losing rations in the counting of noses. He could not keep his children from the white man's school. He could not hunt enough to do without the cotton shirts and overalls from the agencies. Many could not even avoid the white man's names that came to those who were baptized in his church: John, William, Peter, names that meant nothing.

Yet there was one thing that fascinated Yellow Bird, the iron horse that rolled to the horizon on its iron road. How big was the earth? Did the white man own it all, from great water to great water, all but that small part still held by his people? And what of the white Grandmother who was said to rule beyond the great water to the east, whose land in the north he had visited as a boy? All these questions drew Yellow Bird as a moth to the flame, and yet he knew what the moth lacked sense to know, that the flame would kill. But would it? Perhaps, instead, it would give him strength, as fire was said to forge the weapons of the white man.

He did not know the answers, he only knew the People needed Sitting Bull. If he ever returned, Yellow Bird expected he would be as bad as Red Cloud, who, with his fierce wrinkled face and bleary eyes, sat on the bluff above his agency like a deposed king. He lived in a white man's house stuffed to the rafters with white men's goods: brassbound trunks, a Franklin stove with no fire inside it, a machine that sewed cloth as fast as ten squaws, and a sway-backed bed, brass-knobbed and square as the alien building that contained it. Red Cloud was old, and the days of his glory were old days, but other paper chiefs were being raised up to depose Sitting Bull. There was John Grass, who looked like a white man from behind. There was Gall, a warrior once, leader of braves on the Greasy Grass but now the white man's trot-along, receiving white man's gold every year for confiscated ponies he had never owned. With such leaders, the old ways were lost, and Yellow Bird wished to shout to whatever spirit powers there were left in the world that this was wrong beyond enduring.

When Sitting Bull finally returned, he rode a white horse and wore a white sombrero big around as a tepee. Both were gifts from Buffalo Bill, and it seemed at first that the chief had indeed gone the way of Red Cloud, as Yellow Bird had expected. Buffalo Bill was a good man, Sitting Bull told them, but Yellow Bird was reassured to hear that he had no more trust in white men than before. The fire wagon had not taken him to the home of the white chief in Washington as he had expected, and only after he had spoken to a hissing crowd of whites, telling them that his fighting days were over and that he wished to shake hands with their Great Father, was he informed that his translator had altered his words into a bloodthirsty gloating over the slaughter of Long Hair Custer and his bluecoats. Twice this had happened. No more would he speak through a white man's twisted mouth, nor would he return again to the white man's land or visit the Grandmother across the great water as Buffalo Bill wanted. "There is talk of the white men taking more of our land. I must stay here." But he urged others to go. They would learn much from the white man, and such knowledge would be helpful in resisting his magic and cunning.

To be surrounded by that vast pallid tribe which he so adamantly hated occurred to Yellow Bird only in dreams. When Sitting Bull called him to his lodge, shared a pipe, and suggested that he volunteer to join Buffalo Bill Cody's Wild West Show, Yellow Bird felt the hair lift upon the back of his neck. "I have thought, one day, you would be as great as Worm. These Wasichu have come from the east, bringing the daybreak star of understanding. They have made a great world. I have seen it. You are young and may learn much: how to bring the sacred hoop together, how to make the holy tree bloom once again. We have spoken of your vision of the red road. Who is to say it does not lead toward the dawn star?"

"No!" Yellow Bird replied, making the cut-off sign. He would not speak of it. For three days he brooded alone while others volunteered. To be adrift among white men repelled him, and yet, as the prospect smoldered in his brain, it fascinated. From their land much evil came, and some good that was beyond understanding. As men, they were less hearty than his people, starved more easily, wilted more quickly under the summer sun, stiffened with the winter cold. But the whites had magic that made them powerful, magic of the black book, magic of the singing wire and the iron horse: the magic his people needed to hold their land. This was his chance to seek that magic out. It might not come again.

So on the third day Yellow Bird left his lodge and pulled the cross-sticks over the closed flap. A man's lodge was sacred. No one would enter. He took little with him—the clothes on his back, his medicine bag, his bow and arrows, and the live stone from the Greasy Grass that told the white man's time. Time, like the sun, kept its dial in his brain, and for years the live stone had puzzled him. Those little black hands, one that moved quickly pointing its finger, the other shorter, tired, scarcely moving at all, had confused him. What could they have to do with the rising and setting of the sun? Yet they must have, for each day when the sun was high, for a moment they both pointed toward that small turning knob which he took to represent the sun. They seemed to tell the bell of the white man's chapel when to chime and the bugler when to sound his call. He took this watch as protection against the Wasichu and went to meet the wagons that came from Rushville and the iron road.

The fire wagon called to them even before Yellow Bird could see it, and that howling from beyond the hill made him shiver. It was a warning, a death chant for the old days. From the rise he saw the endless iron road, the long black god, that eater of wood which belched sparks from its red mouth. The People had dragged one down once. Now they were dancing beside the iron road in its honor, dressed in full war paint. It seemed to be all in fun, but hate smoldered hot inside Yellow Bird as the fire licked within the body of the iron horse.

When the dancing was over, a tall man in a snow-white suit with a beard sharp as a lance head made a speech of welcome. His last words were spoken in the tongue of the Sioux People. That surprised Yellow Bird, and it was with lessened anxiety that he climbed aboard the first iron wagon. Inside, it was thickly upholstered, its walls painted with pictures of wounded animals, strange creatures he had never seen. This was how it must be in Red Cloud's house, and, feeling an odd pleasure that he did not like, Yellow Bird sat down. Then a man in uniform, babbling about "Zulu cars," moved them on with flapping arms as though he were driving stock until they came to a car with facing benches of bare, hard wood and a straw-covered floor.

"This zoo . . . loo car," he said, pointing all around. "Zulu car for you. For Indian. Savvy?"

Yellow Bird savvied all right: windows sealed with rusty nails, air reeking of sweaty white bodies not long departed, soot-blackened coal stove—the sort of leftovers Indians always got. His body rebelled against touching any of it. They all stood like bewildered cattle until the train, with a nightmarish howl, leaped forward and settled them in sprawling heaps. Some stayed where they were. A few slept, or pretended to. One sang his death song.

Outside, the prairie ran away from them, slowly gathering speed. Yellow Bird edged toward the exit. He had formed no conscious resolve, but his body urged him to escape. Others responded only with their eyes. A few, as though magnetized, followed, but even as Yellow Bird raised his hand toward the latch, the door swung inward and the tall man in the white suit pushed through. He filled the frame with muscle, bone, and gristle, but it was not the size of him or his blade-shaped beard that caught and held. It was the eyes. Eyes like that could count a man's vertebrae from the front. He placed a hand on Yellow Bird's shoulder. Smilingly he turned him around until both of them faced the others. "How." The white man greeted them in their own tongue. "I see old friends here. Lame Elk, Running Water, it is good to have you back. I've heard good reports about some others. Yellow Bird and Elk Standing, I want you to think of me as your father. My name is Bill. Some call me Buffalo Bill. Soon you will see strange things, things that may be beyond understanding. Come to me and I will explain them to you. I will be your father in these things of the white man's land."

He talked on, picturing the great villages they would see, the important chiefs for whom they would perform. Yellow Bird, with the weight of that white arm upon his shoulder, thought grimly, "I should kill him, this one who is named for the buffalo he has killed." Yet all the while another voice argued within him, "This white man has no bad heart against the People. He speaks with a straight tongue." By the time

Buffalo Bill had finished, the windows of the Zulu car had turned dark with evening and the train was going very fast.

The car's one flickering oil lamp gave little light. The lulling sway, the whisper of crumpled newspaper settled sleep upon the car. Not for Yellow Bird. He stood between the cars, where he heard occasional snoring from the white car ahead. No Indian would make such a telltale noise in the night; it would have been trained out of him as a baby. He watched the passing of the high plains, silver under the moon. By the time they reached the prairies, they were going so fast he wondered if the one who lashed on the iron horse had fallen asleep. They hurtled down a steep grade and swung around a long curve. With a memory of torn-up rails in his brain, Yellow Bird stood alert, half ready to jump.

Toward dawn the train slowed, throwing up great exhausted billows of smoke, calling out to the lonely darkness. Finally it stopped to hiss and creak at a siding in Long Pine. A few clapboard buildings staggered away down a dusty street. That was all, but it was Yellow Bird's first town. He was not impressed with it, or with the wagonload of salt pork and lukewarm black medicine the whites called coffee which a tipsy, sleepy-eyed stationmaster finally produced after harsh words from Buffalo Bill.

The first weak tincture of dawn was in the sky as the train moved out. It was raining when they reached Omaha. There the wide streets oozed red mud, and wagons churned them constantly. Buffalo Bill Cody led those Indians who chose to disembark down a plank sidewalk. "This is nothing," he told them, making the cut-off sign. "Stay behind me, and keep in line. This is no village to get lost in. It is said the white man has no god west of the Missouri, and that's where we are.

Don't get lost. Keep away from the firewater. It will make you sick. And keep away from the women. They're worse than the firewater." Looking down from holes in the wooden buildings were the sun-dried faces of women. They watched the parade go by with dull eyes, and Yellow Bird needed no one to tell him to keep away. These women smoked pipes like great chiefs. They were men, with the faces of women only.

In the wet street, men passed, dressed not in the blue to which Yellow Bird was accustomed, but in butternut brown. Their heavy boots were made heavier by the sucking mud, and their beards were stained by tobacco. "Keep in line, boys. You will see much better than this." They were passing river-front warehouses, which drooped under the downpour like old abandoned ponies. Yellow Bird had heard that white men raised up great villages, but here there was only ugliness. He felt no regret when the train moved on, nor when he heard that it would clear the next village, Chicago, by night. He awoke as they passed through, and he saw the tall silhouettes of buildings. Like canyon walls, they rose on either side and were pierced here and there by faint light. Indians were said to dwell in such a way, one family upon another, far to the south.

The next two days Yellow Bird saw no end of villages, and of squared-off fields with animals penned inside. What was the strength in this squared world of the white man? He was filled with doubts, for he had always believed that everything changed except the earth, and here it too was altered. Their first real stop was to be New York, the city of which Sitting Bull had spoken with wonder, and they came to it at dusk. Yellow Bird craned his neck to look out of the window at those great buildings of stone which could never be moved, which must stand in their filth forever. Once he was in the street, his ears were assailed with shouts, horns, the clang of metal on metal. There was a brightness in the night that erased the stars. These lights, it was said, were made with the power of thunder. Perhaps that was the secret power of the Wasichu. Perhaps they had enslaved the thunder people.

Lost in body and soul, Yellow Bird clung to the others, and especially to the man in the white suit who led them to the great stone lodge where they would stay. With the others, Yellow Bird smelled it out, like a dog in new surroundings. He resisted entering a small box, but did so finally when those who had been before laughed at him. He clapped his lips tight against fear as the box rose beneath his feet. It opened again on a long closed corridor set with tasseled lamps and tables with legs like eagles, their talons clutching glass balls. He touched one of the feet. Only wood, but still it was stranger than dreaming. Then some Omaha and Pawnee braves appeared and playfully pretended to take coup on the blundering newcomers. They were like long-lost relations.

An arrow rattled off the wall, but before a real melee could begin, Buffalo Bill Cody stepped out of the rising box with a cigar fuming between his teeth. He had a bag of sweet rocks in one hand and a bucket of sweeter snow in the other. "I don't want any more firewater up here," he told them, doling out the candy and ice cream. Yellow Bird mixed them together, and it was the first Wasichu food he had enjoyed. Did snow fall that way for the white man, he wondered?

Cody was speaking again. "Now, you braves who have been here before, you know better than to bring firewater into this lodge. And you new men, some of you haven't even tasted the stuff. Well, you're lucky. It isn't good for white men, and it's worse for you. Your fathers and grandfathers made a mistake welcoming my grandfathers, and they lost their land and their buffalo and got nothing back but a black book, the measles, and a barrel of spirit water. That's right. You were robbed, and maybe now you're saying to yourselves, never listen to a white man. That's fair, too. But I'm telling you, it may be too late to get back what your fathers gave away, but it's not too late to do your people good. You can be big chiefs when you go home. With you people it's always been the strong over the weak. With us, it's been the rich over the poor. You can be rich, if you work hard, and keep away from bad women and firewater." As before, this white man seemed to speak true, and Yellow Bird was puzzled by what seemed an enigma. He had expected white contempt, and this might well be the subtlest trap of all. He must stay on his guard.

All night there was shouting and tumult outside the great lodge. Perhaps that was the secret; the white man never slept. Frequently Yellow Bird went to the window and looked down, and with the first yellow smudge of dawn he had not slept either. The cup of black medicine helped to restore him. "What is this?" he asked. "What has the white man done to this four-legged?" He held up a strip of bacon. The taste was good but strange. Stranger still was the powdery sweet bread with the hole shot through the middle. He ate six of these.

Then they were herded out again into the big cobbled path full of carts and wagons and horses bigger than he had ever seen. What did they feed such horses? Perhaps the shot-through bread had blown them up like that with gas.

"Look!" One of the Pawnee veterans was pointing something out to the newcomers. "See the big lodge? Madison Square Garden," he intoned with all the solemnity of a diplomatic message.

Inside, the big lodge smelled of sweat and dampness. It smelled of four-leggeds, some of which were familiar and re-assuring to Yellow Bird's nose, like the horse and the bear, and others of which were alien, smelling sweetly dangerous. In the great circle of sawdust, big enough to accommodate a small village, they were to prepare for the white crowd that would come later. "Rehearse" was the word. He tried to learn it, but quickly forgot. It was all a game, pretending the way things never really were, with soft-tipped arrows and guns loaded only with powder. White men in red and blue uniforms beat on drums and puffed up their cheeks as they blew through strange metal tubes, like the bugles of the bluecoats, but bigger and more twisted. They played what one of the Pawnees called "The Star-Spangled Banner," and Yellow Bird remembered hearing it at the agency. He would find out later that it was played before each performance, and the whites, in the wooden sit-down-cliffs that reached to the shadowy rafters, always stood and put their hands on their hearts.

Afterward the arena grew black. Before the man-made dawn, a soft tom-tom beat like a heart. Faintly a bugle sounded. Two camps of Indians pretended to sleep. In the first weak glow of a spotlight, one camp arose and performed a war dance on tiptoe. Yellow Bird lay still with the sleepers, those who would be attacked, and he yearned to turn things about, to join with this mock foe and lead a scramble up into the wooden cliffs, to take a few scalps for realism. Each time he fought and lost, then came alive once more to hunt a papier-mâché buffalo and fill it full of arrows, firing from under the belly of his pony. At least the pony was real, with gunpowder in its heels. With his legs locked tight, he could ride a pony like that right up

[122]

through the crowd to the rafters, to where the fake sun was shining.

Once the buffalo was down and dragged away and the Deadwood coach was successfully held up, Buffalo Bill in his glowing white would do his trick shooting. Dr. W. F. Carver would shoot at bottles and pine cones and never miss. But the best of them was the little squaw, Annie Oakley. Yellow Bird wondered at the magic in her eye and in her rifle, which could nip the ash from Cody's Bull Durham cigar or pluck a penny from between her husband's fingers. He'd examined the rifle once and found no special charms such as the guiding eye that some braves chiseled upon the barrels of their guns. He could not look that closely at the white woman's eyes. The magic must all have been there. She must have a bond with eagles.

A cyclone ended the performance. It was Yellow Bird's task to haul on ropes concealed inside a tepee so that the canvas cone would seem to twist violently in the gust and collapse. He ended each performance under a pile of sticks and canvas, sometimes wondering whether the audience really thought they had witnessed a day in the life of his people. More often he did not think at all, but just waited for the place to clear out, so that he could leave the sawdust and the smell of animal sweat, popcorn, and taffy that was becoming for him the sweet sick scent of the white world.

Stranger than the smell was the squareness of the white world. Lodges, paths, all were squared off with sharp corners, defying the vitality of the eternal round. Yellow Bird walked for hours, half-expecting the city to collapse from sheer fatigue much as had happened in the Wasichu holy book. The paths were hard. No grass grew. The faces that passed him on foot, in horse cars, under parasols, or over dark neckchokers were frowning, full of serious intent.

One day he found himself adjusting his expression to meet this purposefulness. He walked faster, caught his toe on a cobblestone, and fell flat. A cart nearly rolled over him, and a voice from the curb said, "Soakers, every last one of 'em." He scrambled to his feet and looked at the man, whose words he did not understand. "Sorry, redskin, I didn't mean it," the man babbled on, still unintelligibly, but assessing more accurately the look in Yellow Bird's eyes than he had the state of his sobriety. Yellow Bird strode on, his pride not allowing him to limp, though his knee hurt. There was nothing really damaged except the ticking stone. Its heart had stopped. Just as well. He had always been a little afraid of it, more so now that he realized how its kin ruled in the land of the white man. In many shop windows he saw small ones, with little faces and hands. On walls and steeples were greater ones with booming bells, all telling the white man when he must elbow through the street, when he must eat and sleep. They made each day a mechanical thing.

Yet clocks were not the whole explanation, and he kept on exploring, seeking out the reason for the white man's power. He discovered markets where ships unloaded great barrels, big enough to pitch a lodge inside. Farther on were tall brick houses, soot-encrusted, splitting at the seams, seeming to stand erect only by leaning on their neighbors. Surely a fervent beating on a tom-tom or one flourish from the cowboy band at the Garden would bring them rattling down into the filthy streets.

In a green square he saw gray and white birds being fed by old women. He looked for snares and saw none. There would

have been vultures and eagles and wild turkeys in the Black
Hills. From a round mesh basket, which he thought was made
strong as a trap for the birds, he plucked a paper covered with
dark talking signs. He held it at arm's length like a rattler. He
did not want his distrust of it to show, so he returned it to the
basket only after studying pictures of lodges, people in car-
riages, and Buffalo Bill on horseback. Here everything was a
show, the Pawnee had told him. They had spoken of the
curious square look-in-holes in all the lodges through which
Yellow Bird watched the white people working, eating, and
talking with one another. Sometimes they laughed back at him,
or shouted. Now and then a shade was pulled down, and it was
not long until he realized the Pawnee were wrong about the
look-in-holes. Always the questions arose thicker than answers.
Why did the white men treat their women as pets? Why did
the children seem to be either toys or little enemies? He himself might eat a camp dog if he were hungry, but he would not
treat it with such disrespect.

He found the city better at night. He had grown used to the
crash and boom of traffic. Lamps glowed everywhere so that
he could hardly tell if the moon were rising or another lamp
had been hung in the sky. That was the great puzzlement. Here
everything was man-made. It was as though the mother earth
no longer mattered. He had to walk blocks to find a tree or
a patch of soil and then it was fenced in. Here somewhere lay
the key to the white man's power, but where? If it was in the
overcoming of nature and the turning of it into something
other than what it had been meant to be, then he did not want
it. The price was too high.

He had not puzzled it out during the mild winter of fog and
freezing rain, nor during the Moon of Light Snow when Cody

told them the show was leaving New York. They would go east, across the great water to the homeland of the Grandmother. Their great canoe, the *State of Nebraska*, waited for them at a moldering wharf on the Hudson River. Stagecoaches, horses, all were driven into the canoe's vast belly. Yellow Bird wrapped his blanket around him and clutched the rail as they sailed on the morning tide. Tugs hooted and butted against the ship like thirsty puppies around their milky mother. The cowboy band struck up "Yankee Doodle" while Buffalo Bill Cody stood on the bridge. His pale hair was a banner in the breeze as he lifted his hat to the hard blue sky. They were off with a demon's cry from the tall black stack, and Yellow Bird felt an odd stirring inside him like the time he had tried firewater. Perhaps it was a sign of visions to come, of revelations for the sake of his people that he had not yet had in the land of the Wasichu.

Before evening the land had vanished. Yellow Bird watched the hunter stars on the horizon as they began the great circle of the night, and he felt reassured by the roundness of all. The sharp-edged world was left behind, but so much water frightened him. It frightened them all, Indians and cowboys alike. Thinking of the edge where the sky and sea met, some braves sang their death songs.

That night no one showed them how the hammocks worked, so Yellow Bird and the others in his cabin tried to sleep on the rolling floor. The ship never rested. The ceiling, walls, and floor murmured and groaned and pipes gurgled, apparently enduring the same digestive difficulties that he felt rising within himself. Seen in the first light of dawn, the waves were angry and fuming. When Yellow Bird tried to walk the deck he progressed with enormous downhill lurches, then with a series of wavering uphill steps. His hands fluttered like an amateur on a tightrope until he landed against the rail. Below, the ocean boiled, lifted toward him, sank away until something inside him rose in sympathy. From then on he heard nothing, saw nothing, not even the sailors who laughed at him. He was all sickness in a shifting, sliding world where he and his people would never be at home.

By day's end the storm grew worse. There was no laughter now. The sailors ran to lash things down. Waves leaped up, dark and more ominous than the hills of home. Those who were still able dressed for death, pulled blankets up above their eyes. "Eyia-ah-ah, O Powers, save us. Powers of the storm that live in all the directions, save us." Yellow Bird prayed over and over. Toward dawn of the second day the winds slackened, though the waves continued to leap at them with snapping jaws. A few of the show's buffalo and elk had died in the night. Sailors dragged the carcasses on deck and flung them over, and Yellow Bird wept for them because they would never return, never touch the earth again.

The days on the great water merged one into another. Yellow Bird began eating again, though the food sat heavy in his throat. They would all die here. Even the passing glimpse of land, which he was told was Ireland, did not reassure him. Then at a place called Gravesend a hungry little tug came out to greet them. It flew the American flag and sent jets of water arching into the sky. When its band struck up "The Star-Spangled Banner," a few braves who had heard it through endless opening ceremonies lifted their voices in droning chorus. Yellow Bird kept silent. When the time came, he would sing his own song.

On that final night before disembarking, Buffalo Bill was

all pressed, manicured, and shaved, for the public had come to him. He was brimming with plans for London, and one expressly involved Yellow Bird.

"I have been thinking about you, my son," Buffalo Bill began, paternal as always. "You have strange hair. It is not black like the hair of your people. Why, I ask?"

"It comes from the Powers," Yellow Bird replied.

"That is true of all things, Yellow Bird. Did your mother have yellow hair?"

"Her hair was as black as the raven's wing."

"Your father?"

"I do not remember him," Yellow Bird lied. "He died many winters ago."

"My son, your face begins to grow whiskers, like a white man's. Don't look that way. Whiskers are natural and proper. I can see you with a beard like a prophet out of the black book. Let it grow. Let it grow under your nose, a mustache like General Custer's. You know, with a mustache you would look like old Long Hair."

"No!" Yellow Bird denied it fiercely.

"Why such a loud no, Yellow Bird? Do our minds think together? I have heard a story about Custer and an Indian princess."

"No!"

"Do not be angry with me, Yellow Bird. I have been thinking of putting you in a play, on a stage. How would you like to be the most important person in the story? Big picture outside, with you on it, and letters so these English people can read it. 'Son of Custer' it would read."

"I am not what you say I am."

"Bags of money. You'll go home a rich Indian, buy yourself a herd of ponies, a good woman, a princess."

Yellow Bird turned his back.

"Look at me, son. I'm thinking of you. You may not like it, but you're part Wasichu. It's as plain as the nose on your face. If you won't listen to me, see what a mirror tells you. It's not your fault, but it would be stupid"—and here Buffalo Bill tapped his forehead for emphasis—"stupid for you not to use it. Think about it. We'll work up a good show. Great big sign, 'The Life and Death of Yellow Bird.' You like that better?"

Yellow Bird said nothing. He would rather die than play his father. Yes, he would die, and not alone. All the way up to London, in a coach surrounded by cheering crowds, he brooded upon it. He was back among the squared-off sharp edges, far from the round solitude of his home.

Almost against his will, for he hated to take any of Buffalo Bill's advice, he glared at himself later that day in a mirror. A ghost stared back at him. "My father," he said. For a long time the images considered one another with hate and sorrow. Then for a while Yellow Bird tormented his chin with a pair of tweezers, pulling out that first damning trace of hair. There was no end to it, nor would he admit that he must shave with a razor as white men did. In the end, he flung open the window and hurled the mirror into the darkness. Silence, a sound of shattering glass four flights below, and then a stringing out of words, curses in which the white man specialized. Yellow Bird slammed the window down. Just let him come up. If the mirror hadn't scalped him, Yellow Bird was ready to finish the job.

The first London performance was given for the Prince and Princess of Wales. Afterward there was talk of the Grandmother attending and of certain white chiefs from Europe riding on the stagecoach during the holdup scene. Buffalo Bill gave them a speech about good conduct. When the Grandmother came, they must be gentle. They must act as though she were their own grandmother, but for the princes they could seem as fierce as they pleased. Then, if all went well, the tour might continue through all the capitals of Europe. He had a special word for Yellow Bird. Rehearsals for the Custer act were soon to begin. Possibilities were unlimited. Posters were already being drawn up. Yellow Bird had seen them, and he had noted the reserve in the eyes of his fellow braves.

It was after the close of the first Wild West show that he found himself standing before the chest that contained the arms for the stagecoach scene. The chest was unlocked, and he found his hands grasping the lid, then withdrawing, one after another, the six carbines within, manipulating the levers, which spilled out one blank cartridge after another, and in their stead inserting live brass and lead. He did not work fast. If he were discovered, let it be. If the consequences started a war between the white nations or simply ended the tour, let that be as well. The Powers would decide, not he. No one came. He lowered the lid on the loaded weapons and snapped home the lock. His part was done. As the Powers had directed his hands, let them now direct the flight of the bullets.

The next day the royal box was prepared. There was a crowd waiting in the street, and the roar of it shouting "Jubilee, Jubilee" preceded the Grandmother like the sea against the shore. When she came in sight, her great coach drawn by eight buckskin horses glittered like the morning star. She is beyond the touch of bullets or arrows, thought Yellow Bird. They would flatten against her dress and fall to the ground. When the show began, a soldier carried in the flag and dipped it to the Queen. She bowed to the flag, and when the performers entered, Yellow Bird among them, they brought no weapons, only their songs and their dances. The guns remained locked in their boxes, for this was a gentle lady with no love of violence.

When the performance ended, Red Shirt, who called himself a chief and looked like one, was presented to the Queen. He strode forward with the dignity of one ruler encountering another and about to sign a treaty of lasting peace and friendship. He spoke for the Indians, and then the Queen told them all, "I am sixty-eight years old. I have traveled all over the world and seen every sort of people, but today I have seen the handsomest people I know. If you were my subjects, I would not let them take you about in a show." Then she shook hands with the chief and after him with all the others. Yellow Bird found her hands soft and small, and her worried little face was pale with the blueness of live things found under stones. She hid her power and wisdom well, he thought, this tiny, timid old woman who commanded so great a tribe.

What that show lacked in noise and violence they were to make up for the following day. Then the Kings of Saxony, Greece, and Denmark, and the Crown Prince of Austria, all of whom had come to England to honor Victoria's Jubilee, would take part. They would ride in the old Deadwood coach, and Yellow Bird was among those Indians who would give chase. The orchestra began with "The Star-Spangled Banner," as always. "I will not have to hear that tune again," thought Yellow

Bird. From the weight of it, he felt sure he'd been handed
one of the loaded guns. The scene in the hunters' camp followed the orchestra, and then, with the spotlights roving overhead, came the jostling Deadwood coach, full to the brim with
kings. Red Shirt sounded the barking cry of attack. The ponies
leaped forward into the dazzle of lights. Ahead, the coachman
whipped up his horses. Once around they went, pursued and
pursuer, with the crowd standing. The spotlights swept down
and around, a confusion of colors. Dust flew high, spun from
the wheels and flung back by flying hoofs, and then the first
carbine was leveled, the first shot was fired.

For Yellow Bird it was a hammer blow, a spine-prickling
call to attention. The coach fired back, the soft blue cloud of
a shotgun loaded with black powder and a wad of paper. He
could not bring his finger to pull the trigger. Around they went
again, always gaining, the coach a growing blue ahead of them.
No, he could not fire. Let the Powers decide all. They were
just behind the coach now. Guns went off at close range. From
somewhere in the darkness Yellow Bird thought he heard a cry
of surprise and pain, and then it was again time for the kings
to fire back, with their useless revolvers filled with blank cartridges. It was time to fall from his pony into the banked sawdust. It was time to pretend to die, and Yellow Bird went
down almost wishing the lead were inside him.

So the Indians were beaten off as they always were beaten
off, the stagecoach lumbered on to the dark thunder of the
crowd. Once more the white man had won, but what of the
live bullets? Where had they lodged? Yellow Bird rose from
the sawdust and took his bow with the others. The audience
cheered on the losers and he saw nothing unusual. Squinting
into the raised fire from the lamps, he saw no huddling group,

no one being carried away. Presently the kings reappeared in their box, paler, perhaps, but smiling, taking their bows. The show went on with Buffalo Bill in the center ring, his white coat incandescent as a moon moth caught in firelight. Then a stagehand approached him, leaned close, and whispered something in his ear. Yellow Bird saw the blood drain from Bill's ruddy face as though one of the vagrant bullets had finally found him.

In a way, it had. When the show was over, they were called together into the darkened arena, the half-dozen Indians who had attacked the coach, by the tall white man who stood before them holding a lantern. "One of you is a lucky redskin," Bill Cody began, his voice hoarse from shouting during the show. "One of you. Maybe all of you know what I'm talking about." He walked around the half circle holding the lantern high, staring into each face. Some let their eyes drop, studied their feet. Yellow Bird gazed back. What did it matter? He did not blink, though Buffalo Bill's eyes tried to suck the soul from his body. "One of you, maybe all of you, won't be surprised to hear that the Deadwood coach is full of holes. Bullet holes. Why? I don't smell firewater." No Indian replied. Bill studied Yellow Bird closely, as one might examine a puzzle to see if it had too few pieces or too many. "Some of your people are going home before this show moves on. Do any of you wish to go with them?" Again silence. "Well, if no one will speak, I have no choice. All of you will go home."

With this he dismissed them, holding back only Yellow Bird. "I am unhappy," he said. "I thought of you as my son. I thought you had a future with this show. But part of you inside is twisted. Which part, Yellow Bird? The white or the red? I know you will not speak out. But you are the one. I feel it here." He touched his breast while Yellow Bird stood stolidly. A corpse would have more readily replied. "Yes, you are the one. I'd like to straighten you out. I'm used to handling big snakes. But the little ones that crawl up and sting you in the back . . . I don't like that kind. Go on, pack your bag. There's a ship for New York in the morning."

A dozen Indians were on it, the six who stood accused, two with coughing sickness, one who could not say no to firewater, and the others despondent in a world they had not made and could not comprehend. The weather was fair, the trip slow. One of the despondent Indians died in his blankets. No one knew until he began to smell, and that was in New York harbor. From New York they went as they had come, by rail, and the fare used up nearly all the money they had left. Yellow Bird stood long on the rear platform watching the fields and houses of the white world shrink behind him. He saw the posthole diggers driving their spears into the nape muscles of the mother earth, watched her being conquered, dug into, shaped in the white man's image. He saw the wild land retreating before the roads and the iron rails that followed the lost pathways of the deer and the Indian. He saw it all, less with remorse than with a growing persuasion that he could not fight the white man; not alone, without allies or special powers. When even the Powers would not assist him, there was no use trying.

Nearly a year had passed since Yellow Bird had been home. After the majesty of London, the vastness of the ocean, and the grinding weight of New York, the village at Pine Ridge looked tiny and drab, crushed against the earth. Buffalo hides were gone from the lodges. Dim light glowed through unpainted canvas walls. Buckskin had nearly disappeared as clothing. The People wore cast-off shirts, overcoats, and trousers from the agency store. As surely as the buffalo shed their coats in spring, they were changing, becoming as the white man, with no season strong enough to turn them back again. Nor was it an accident, but rather something the white man pushed upon them, like the new belfry-topped boarding school. There the children were taught to forget the old stories and the old songs. They learned to live by the bells that rang out the demanding pace of white man's time. Time was a disease with the white man, who lived not by the seasons but by the tiny ticking of a metal heart. Yellow Bird knew that ticking; he had even heard the terrible doomsday booming of the great father of clocks that stood in London. Time had become an infection in his own blood. It was an awareness which chopped the solid days into tiny grains that spilled away too fast.

So Yellow Bird listened to the bells and bugles of the white man's world and despaired for them all, feeling as helpless as the fat squaw who had tried to hang herself. Fearing that she would be obliged to drag it through eternity, she had chosen the smallest tree possible for a gallows, and her attempt had broken the thin trunk. Now she had nothing to show for her trouble but a bruised backside.

There was no hope for his people in what Yellow Bird saw, only the black and empty road. He was afraid of their mortality. So many had betrayed him by dying that it seemed better to love the eternal mountains, the storms that whispered of better days, without saying how or when. Rather than skulk in a canvas agency lodge, Yellow Bird gave what money he had left for an unbroken pony and headed into the wilds. He watched constantly for buffalo, not only to feed and clothe himself, but as a sign that there was hope for the return of the old ways. Once he thought he saw a herd's breath cloud the frosty morning air. He rode recklessly toward it, but only a train chugging west came into sight. The circling flock of blackbirds, which once would have signaled that they were feeding on grasshoppers stirred up by many hoofs, turned out to be only a raid on a freshly seeded field.

The buffalo were gone. What he had long feared he now saw with his eyes. Even the buzzards wheeling on the wind failed to show him where the buffalo were. Only the white bones remained and these, too, were vanishing. Penniless grangers and bankrupt hunters came with their oxcarts and loaded up bones for meal and china, horns for buttons and combs, hoofs for glue. There were Indians among the hunters, who fired the prairies so that the white bones would stand out more clearly. It was one of these who set his grass fire too close to a nest of rattlesnakes and turned Yellow Bird himself into a bone hunter. The grass fire still smoldered when Yellow Bird arrived, but the snakes had done their job and the hunter had set his last fire. His ponies stood by, heads drooping, already hitched to a half-loaded wagon. This Yellow Bird filled from the charred field with the bones that the fire had not spoiled.

Before dusk the wagon was heaped high, and the next day he followed a slow caravan of Indian bone hunters. Blanket-wrapped, clad in agency cotton, they drove slowly toward the railhead. Ungreased carts groaned. Dogs yelped at first, but the dust and the miles stifled them, and it was a silent, funereal procession that finally halted to pitch camp within sight of the railhead. The wagons rolled on to the weighing station. Eight dollars a ton, take it or leave it. Yellow Bird studied the four silver dollars in his hand. The bits and pieces of how many buffalo, he wondered, had made him rich enough to get soundly drunk.

Before returning, he walked once around the waiting pile of bones. Twice the height of a man, it stretched for a quarter of a mile along the railhead. It was a picture that stayed in his mind that night as he lay looking up through branches at the darkening sky. He saw the bones behind his lids, looked up again where a high wind lashed the leaves, shut his eyes, and finally slept. Then he saw them again in a dream, connecting one to another, becoming whole animals, a mighty lowing herd upon which white hunters descended. When they fired their long-range guns, it was the hunters who fell, immediately becoming worm-covered skeletons. In the dream, the wind stirred the bones and played music through them. When he awoke, or thought he did, to that weird music it sounded more like the rushing overhead of a flight of geese. At first he saw nothing. No breeze stirred in the dull dawn light. Then he saw it emerging through the trees and vanishing again, a figure moving his way, ethereal as morning mist exhaled from the damp earth.

I'm dreaming, he thought, or if I'm not, it's a ghost. What he saw, men talked about but few saw in a lifetime, not even the old men who could still remember when it was good to be alive. All of the early light seemed condensed around the huge shape as though it were the source: a white buffalo, gone almost before Yellow Bird was sure of what he had seen. Overhead, the comprehending birds were silent. Yellow Bird rose to his feet and ran to his pony, a stolid animal that never had startled at the growl of a grizzly or the scent of blood. It stood now wide-eyed, hind legs spread, ready to rear or leap away, and he had to soothe it with words about its great courage and about the exploits of other famous ponies that would live forever in song.

Finally mounting, Yellow Bird was surprised to find a trail —great U's cut deep and clear in the soft soil. When he saw it again, the white buffalo was not hurrying. It tilted its tremendous horns forward to avoid the low branches. He followed at a walk into the misty sunlight, where it lingered on a hillside, unfrightened, master of the morning. He lost it once in the dazzle of the sun's arising, then heard it again before he saw it. A cry of dumb yearning came from its uplifted, moon-eyed head. He was close enough now to see that the eyes were huge, the eyes of a demon or a god. It moved on again, seemed to wait for him to keep up, moved again in the white fume of its own hot breath. Yellow Bird never thought of his carbine. Though white buffalo robes were rare and valued for their beauty and power, he sensed that he must not, could not, kill this creature which seemed to lead him toward some revelation.

His pony, which had gone stiff-legged as though the grass were full of snakes, began to edge sideways, ears laid back, eyes sliding. He placed a hand on its bunched shoulder, and as though his touch were fire, it rose on its hind legs, struck with its forefeet faster than a rattler. Before Yellow Bird could fling himself aside, the horse fell, its feet still working, the hoofs a glitter of wings about his head. A hoof slammed into a tree stump like the crack of a rifle. An instant later Yellow Bird was caught in the shoulder and spun down.

How long he was stunned, he didn't know. It seemed only a second, but when he staggered to his feet the buffalo was gone, not as though it had walked out of sight but as though it had vanished from existence. By then the sun, pierced by crystal arrows, bled red and orange upon the hill, and all around stretched loneliness as wide and undisturbed as the prairie itself. Though he spent the morning looking, the trail of the buffalo vanished on a stony stretch and did not appear again, and he would have given up the entire quest as a dream or fancy had he not found, clinging to a thornbush, a few white strands of hair. These he put into his medicine sack, but they brought little satisfaction. He must find this creature again, no matter how long or how far he had to search.

VI

White Buffalo Trail

The white buffalo had left no trail. Yellow Bird knew that it was no creature to be stalked in the visible world. He felt certain that if he were to encounter the buffalo at all, it would be in that other realm which his heart so regularly beheld. For many hours he stood on high places, wrapped in his blanket, thoughtfully seeking from the earth and the sky answers to his questions. When nature seemed to refuse and he felt himself coaxed away by weariness, he put pebbles between his toes to keep alert. He saw no buffalo, but once, when he had slumped down near sleep, he saw a maiden high in the rocks, singing. Before he could climb to her she became an eagle that flew away with the sunlight sparkling on its wings, so that he knew it was the bird he had seen upon the white man's coins.

Then he knew that he must seek his vision elsewhere. Washing the red paint from his face, he filled Worm's silver-bound pipe with the crumbled leaves of aromatic sage. This he lifted to the Gods and smoked it in the four sacred directions. "Dawn house, evening house, house of the storm cloud, house of the she-pollen and the he-rain, I smoke to you. Speak to me as you once did." He heard only the sound of his blood. Around him, the wilderness had ceased to breathe. It leaned on him with the dry heat of the summer afternoon, tremendous and crushing. Toward evening the storm came, and with it the voices. In the boiling clouds he saw again the sacred tepee sewn with lightning. Swallows swooped ahead of the thunder, which called out its greeting, and, on those sky-devouring clouds, Yellow Bird seemed to see Crazy Horse riding before ghost armies. His hair flew back, his eyes were smoldering coals. This was how he would have looked riding beside Chief Joseph in that last snow-driven fight in the Bear Paw Mountains.

It was not from conjuring storms alone that Yellow Bird's reputation continued to grow. He knew something about herbs from Worm, and he understood the value of boiled water from observing white shamans in New York and London. When Big Foot, the cadaverous old Miniconjou chief whose face was wind-riven beyond ugliness to a kind of stony grandeur, came to him with the coughing sickness, Yellow Bird's status was assured. In fact, he knew little about curing the disease. The whites, he knew, would advise a sea voyage, but that would hardly satisfy the gnarled old chief who had never traveled far from the sacred hills, so with the morning sun boring red through the thin canvas of the mission tepee, Yellow Bird drew the sacred circle on the floor. This he divided into quadrants. He had no faith in rattles or masks to frighten away demons. Rather than magic, he sought a state of harmony with the world, for in harmony there was strength and health. Whether it was the prayers he said, or the herbs given out, or something else beyond telling, Big Foot went away and said he was cured.

Yellow Bird had less success with Crow Foot, Sitting Bull's scowling son, who had from birth walked upon a twisted foot. He hated the white doctor who had offered to cut into the foot with a small bright knife. He was no less scornful of Yellow

Bird and his charms and incantations, but the visits gave Yellow Bird a chance to smoke with Sitting Bull. The red-veined face softened as the tobacco formed a sweet cloud of contentment about his head. "I see power in you," he told Yellow Bird. "I see a light all through your body." Of himself he had only small things to say: that he was no chief, simply a man. He claimed leadership of no tribe, though many resided with him. Toward the whites he harbored little hatred, only suspicion. He lived now in one of their square lodges, but when he traded with them he asked no favors, giving value for value. 'With the white man you must be as careful as the wolf who has lost his foot in a steel trap," he said. "Now I am invited to go again with Buffalo Bill to the land of the Grandmother. They want me away so that Washington can change the treaty and take more of our land."

"No Indian would sign such a paper," Yellow Bird insisted.

"No Indian? What of the shave-heads who are paid to police the reservation?"

"No chief would sign."

"Crow Dog would. They would pay him, and he would sign. There are others. But we will stand against them." Sitting Bull was an old man, who had worn his war bonnet in the teeth of fate for half a lifetime, and the years were like the trimming back of a vine. They had not destroyed him, they had only made him hard. As he stood up, his legs creaked. "Hear them," he said, laughing. "They tell me I am not so young as I think. You and ones like you will have to take my place. It will be harder then."

Harder beyond contemplation. Yellow Bird was already weary of ceaseless searching. He was tired of being strange. All his life he had been a stranger seeking another world, for

there were no people to call his own. Now, in his young manhood, he found a girl. He heard her and her sister before he
saw them. He listened to their silly songs and private laughter
from the lodge next to his own. Deer Walking was her name,
and he had fallen in love with her warm voice on a clear morning in the Month of the Spring Moon when hail and sunshine
mixed together. He saw her first in white buckskin and beads,
fresh as a sprite of springtime, straight as an arrow, as taut
with health as a newly strung bow. As he stood gawking, she
looked at him, eyes dilated, her mouth set in a childish expression of surprise. She seemed to Yellow Bird beautiful beyond
telling, though in time he would realize her fetching expression
had less to do with her innocent soul than with the fact that
her teeth were crooked.

Thus began the courtship of Yellow Bird and Deer Walking, and it was for him more of a trial than his days of vigil
had been. In one way those were easy times for a young man,
since many of his potential rivals had died in the long wars
with the whites and there were more than enough women to
go round. On the other hand, Yellow Bird had special liabil-
ities. He had no family, no ready intermediary, no war honors
or pony herd to sweeten his proposal. Besides, he sensed that
he terrified the girl. For the first time, eating had begun to
bore him. Some days he got along with water and a bit of
dried venison. It was customary to tease girls when they went
to the stream for water, to throw plums or cherries at them,
but Deer Walking looked so alarmed that he wished only to
protect her, to fend off the threat that appeared to be himself. At night, under the fireflies and the restless stars, while
the crickets whirled away the dampness from their wings, he
listened to soft laughter. Drawn by it, he would stand outside

[144]

her lodge, stiff and silent as a mountain cedar. At most she would peek out at him and look startled. Then an old woman would come and laugh or shove him away and he would withdraw to some nearby hill to play his medicine flute. Only when his lips were parched and the moon was down would he moisten a bit of barley cake and eat it, for life must go on.

Growing desperate and thinner than he had been since the last winter in Canada, Yellow Bird went in search of an elk, that beast which was said to have power over women. Three nights of hunting brought him what he wanted, a dead elk at his feet. The carcass he took to Deer Walking's lodge, keeping for himself only the white of one eyeball and the gristle from a hind fetlock. With these charms in his medicine bag, if he could not charm her, he would at least be able to carry her off.

With more optimism than usual, Yellow Bird appeared before Deer Walking's lodge that evening. The flyblown carcass of the elk was all that greeted him at first. As the last colors faded in the west, the old woman emptied a pot full of stale water on his feet as though he did not exist. Yellow Bird went off to play his flute. There was no hope, he decided. She despised him. This conviction wound out through the bony flute and languished in the darkness, but with the rising moon, his melody and spirits picked up. Deer Walking was being held prisoner, he decided. What else could account for so violent a rebuff? His intentions were honorable; they ought to know that by now. If Deer Walking cared as he did, the old people could not stop them any more than they could stop the winter snow from falling or the moon from rising up.

Yellow Bird tried to talk to her at the stream the next morning, but she only stared at him with wide eyes and placed her hand before her mouth as though to stifle an exclamation. While he hesitated, the old woman came creeping down the trail. "If this goes on much longer," he thought, "I shall die of longing and starvation." There was a practice, not altogether frowned upon, of stealing maidens in the night. If he got away with it, the deed would be to his credit. If he were caught, he would be made to look a fool before the tribe. Perhaps, then, this was the way to proceed.

His imagination raced ahead of his actions; he saw himself prowling under the moon, a bright blade gleaming in his right hand. Then he pictured the knife at work, soundlessly cutting a long slit through the side of Deer Walking's lodge. His patience was endless. The blade scarcely moved as the moon set and the sun still slept below the horizon. At last he entered, gathered her up, and fled. He rode with her into the glory of the rising sun, but here his imagination betrayed him utterly. In the darkness of the lodge, he had made a hideous mistake. It was not Deer Walking he held in his arms, but the old woman. He heard her screaming like an eagle, and then he saw Deer Walking's father, Broken Tooth, stumbling after them, brandishing a still-smoking pipe tomahawk. No, never, he decided. There had to be a better way.

After a day of self-criticism and torment, he went to Broken Tooth's lodge with his only valuable possession, his pony. Broken Tooth sat outside the lodge flap with a half-empty bottle of firewater beside him. Yellow Bird tried to present the pony to the old man as a prenuptial gift, but he was waved away for talking foolishness. "He is a very fine pony," Yellow Bird urged. Broken Tooth raised the liquor bottle to his lips, took a long final suck, and then pitched the empty bottle, end over end, in Yellow Bird's general direction. He was too drunk to hit anything.

"He'll sleep well," thought Yellow Bird. "I should come boldly tonight in the dark of the moon. I should come disguised so that if I fail there would be no ridicule. But I do not know how Deer Walking feels. Do I want to take her against her will?" Once there had been a brave named Looking Glass who, failing to win his love, had stripped naked and painted himself from head to foot with the black and red tinctures of the spirit world. Then he had made his way in the dead of night to his maiden's lodge, and cut his way inside. Stealthily he lay down beside her, for he heard her father stirring. Waiting for the old warrior to drift into unconsciousness, Looking Glass himself had fallen asleep. That would not happen to him, Yellow Bird felt sure; his pounding heart would never permit it. In the story, Looking Glass had slept soundly, to be aroused at dawn by a fearful scene. The maiden had discovered a prostrate painted demon beside her. Terrified and confused, Looking Glass had sprung to his feet and fled. He had burst through the dew-sparkling grass and sage on feet that scarcely touched the ground, and had plunged head first into a river nearby. Paint had smoked out behind him as though he were going down in flames.

Yet all had ended happily for Looking Glass. The maiden's father, fearing that a demon desired his daughter, had sought him out immediately. As the lesser of two evils, Looking Glass had been taken as a son-in-law. So the story went, but to Yellow Bird it was all foolishness, nor did he wish to take by force a bride who did not care for him.

That night he could not sleep. "If she will not have me willingly, and if I will not try to steal her away, what then?" Only a fool starves himself to death for love, and so before dawn he had come to a decision. He would go on a hunt, a long one: long enough to forget the taste of the white man's meat; long enough to make a bow that would not break; long enough to deaden the clock that ticked inside his head, seeming to toll away the last spinning days of a world flung out of control. But if the hunt would be long enough to forget Deer Walking he did not know. He left in darkness, the dew softening the soles of his moccasins.

Yellow Bird was away from the agency throughout the summer. Hunting was hard, and what game he found was small. He hoped always to see again the white buffalo, but he saw not even dark ones. The prairies seemed picked clean even of their bones, as though they had never been. Occasionally the thunder spoke to him of sacred trees and the good road. The storm voices urged him on, but to where? The message seemed never complete. When the summer was done, when the cherries had ripened and turned black and the cool moon had come, he had nothing to show for his hunting but a string of three stray ponies, one of them old and sway-backed, another that limped, and his own. This was not much to show for the whole season of hard work.

His lodge had stood through the summer undisturbed, and Broken Tooth's lodge remained beside it. On his first night at home, he lay awake wondering what he should do and listening for the foolish talk and laughter that he had come to love. He heard only Broken Tooth's dyspeptic belch and his methodic cursing in the white man's agency words. In the morning, he found out why. Deer Walking was gone, married to a rich white hunter, Broken Tooth told him.

[148]

"Married," repeated the old woman, hissing like a disturbed tortoise. "Sold for firewater."

"She lies." Broken Tooth's words were slurred together. There were bottles strewn all around his lodge, and beside him on the dusty ground stood a half-empty one. His chin was settled on his chest and he stared up crookedly under heavy brows with an expression combining truculence and despair. "My daughter is well married." He held up the bottle of firewater as if hefting her dowry. Its very color, dark red, seemed somber and important. He stared at the bottle as though he saw a new world within, a place where a man could be quiet and safe.

"Who is this rich hunter, Grandfather?"

"A whiskey seller," interjected the old woman.

Broken Tooth gave her a glance of guilty anger as if to say, "Yes, I've done wrong, but it's your fault, too."

"This one sells his own flesh so he may drink. He is nothing but a dog." Perhaps Broken Tooth had also noted the resemblance. In any case, her words seemed to cut deep, and as she continued to revile him, he turned his head at each thrust as if to make the words glance off. Finished with Broken Tooth, she fixed on Yellow Bird. "The white man of whom this dog speaks looks for a white buffalo. Yes, as you do. He asks everywhere for a guide. I told him you had seen such a buffalo. He pays in gold."

"No."

"The pay, I am told, is good."

"No," Yellow Bird replied again. He had heard of these fancy hunters, some of whom came from across the sea in great gilded wagons, bringing many servants. Some had brought their own orchestras and wore shiny boots with insteps as high as a woman's. "No, I want nothing to do with him."

"It is not Deer Walking's wish to be with this man."

Yellow Bird's shoulders drew together slightly, but he gave no other sign.

"I am afraid for her."

"My ears are closed, Grandmother. I hear nothing you say."

Throughout that day and the next, Yellow Bird kept up the pretense, denying even the existence of the large, red-painted wagon that stood near the agency fort or the slim figure tending the fire beside it. But in the end he found himself gravitating nearer until he finally saw the man, seated on a box, elbows on knees, chin on hands. He looked a thoughtful sort until Yellow Bird drew near. The man was neither large nor brawny, but his neck was thick and corded, making his head seem small. That head was crowned with fiery red hair that jutted up like a rooster's comb. His face, too, had a reddish hue, and his eyes had a rooster's blank stare.

"Well, what's all this," the man said, standing up. "Who are you, redskin?" His voice was as rasping as the stubbles on his chin.

Yellow Bird said his name in English. During his months with the Wild West Show, he had mastered the tongue well enough, although he still had to search his memory for the words to use.

"So you're the one. Well, well." He looked Yellow Bird up and down. "Have a drink, Yellow Bird, and tell me about this white buffalo of yours."

Yellow Bird waved the bottle aside. He felt an automatic antipathy toward this white stranger, as fundamental and beyond examination as the enmity between a wasp and a tarantula.

"That's not very friendly," the man said, taking a drink himself. "Not very Indian of you, neither. But I guess you aren't all Indian, at that, are you? Not with those whiskers. Listen, sit down. My name's Bill Boggs." This seemed to be the truth, judging from a pistol that jutted from his belt, its grip deeply carved, *BB*. Yellow Bird was less convinced by what he said later and by his manner, which seemed too hospitable, too friendly. His every response was an extreme. Humor brought a side-splitting burst of laughter. Interest and enthusiasm made his pale-blue eyes nearly pop from their sockets. Serious concern put a hand to his forehead, pursed his lips. Boggs was a man of self-made fortune, he said. Yellow Bird took him for a cattle rustler, now retired and in search of trophies. He had filled a room with heads and horns and great stuffed fish, he said, but he'd left one place vacant above his fireplace. That was for the last of the buffalo, the white one. He would stop at nothing, he said, until that place was filled. However dishonest his history, however incredible his emotions, Yellow Bird knew that in this at least, Boggs was sincere. The white buffalo would be his guiding star until one or the other was dead.

"I need a tracker," Boggs said, "and the old woman spoke well of you. She said you have seen a white buffalo."

"I saw something," Yellow Bird replied.

"I need you," Boggs said, jingling a leather sack full of coins. "This bag of gold is yours when we take him."

Their interest in the white buffalo gave them a common ground, though no common cause. Boggs wanted it dead, its head upon the wall. Yellow Bird wanted its spirit to live just as passionately as he wanted Crazy Horse and the old days to come again. Then, too, there was Deer Walking. She had kept away until now, and when she saw Yellow Bird, she did not speak except with her eyes. They seemed to shout at him, into him, with a message of alarm.

His conversation with Boggs finally broke off with Boggs setting out his terms and assuming he had hired a guide, and Yellow Bird saying nothing but intending not to return. He did not speak with Deer Walking nor did he seek her out, but later that day she came to him by the stream and spoke openly, as she never had before.

Deer Walking confirmed the old woman's story. She had virtually been sold to Boggs as a wife and cook. Broken Tooth regretted it when he was sober, but was afraid to undo what he had done. Everyone who knew him feared Bill Boggs, and the better they knew him the more they feared.

"He has a wolf's temper," she told Yellow Bird. "He does not always show it, but it is always waiting. When he laughs, that is a bad time."

"Are you asking me to be his guide?"

"Yes. I am afraid. I am afraid when he drinks."

"Why me? Why call on me?"

"If you had only brought the firewater to my father."

"I brought my pony to his lodge."

"He is an old man, too old for hunting."

"How long will this Boggs hunt, do you think?"

"Until the Freezing Moon."

"If I do go . . ."

Deer Walking glowed back at him, and Yellow Bird knew

he was trapped. It was not long before he also knew that he had made a mistake.

They left the following morning. Yellow Bird and Bill Boggs were mounted and Deer Walking drove the wagon, which was fitted inside with the comforts of a white man's lodge.

Yellow Bird dreaded the days, not knowing what he should do if the white buffalo showed itself. He dreaded the nights even more. The thought of those two together in the wagon was like a sharp stone always in the toe of his moccasin, leaving him furious when he rolled in his blanket at night, exhausted and just as angry when he arose in the morning.

Deer Walking could see it. "Don't leave us," she pleaded, observing his tormented eyes. Once, when they were alone, she tried to show him how to smile. She spread his lips with her fingers and in the end he did smile, receiving back beautiful, tormenting laughter.

Such moments were rare. During the daylight hours, Yellow Bird hunted with Boggs. A crack shot, Boggs killed a fine elk and the biggest grizzly Yellow Bird had ever seen, but, after taking a single meal from each, Boggs left the carcasses for the buzzards. There was only one trophy he meant to keep. The evenings were long and hard to bear. Yellow Bird and Deer Walking ate silently while Boggs drank and told of hunts gone by.

Boggs had brought plenty of liquor along, and each night he offered a cup to Yellow Bird and each night Yellow Bird declined, a rebuff Boggs accepted with a shrug. "What's one bottle of whiskey amongst one Boggs?" As the evenings wore on and the bottle was drained, his stories grew wilder, full of dark hints of murdered men and stolen gold. Sometimes he chuckled off register, a crazed sound that made Yellow Bird want to clap a hand over his mouth. Occasionally Boggs interrupted his monologue to criticize Deer Walking—her cooking, the way she kept the wagon, the fact that she was an Indian. In the process, he used words Yellow Bird had never heard one person say to another. Once he struck her. Yellow Bird heard the snap of teeth when the open hand met her chin, saw her raise her own hand to her mouth and let it fall back again.

Yellow Bird felt the blood rise within him. I should take that one's scalp; I should hang it from my tomahawk, he told himself. Yet it was no light thing to interfere between a man and his wife, particularly when that man was white, well armed, and dangerous. This alone would not have kept his knife in its sheath, but there was something more among these three: a band of fascination, a kind of balance sustained by an intangible presence. It seemed to Yellow Bird that the working out of their entwined destinies waited upon the white buffalo.

That was during the first days of the hunt. As time passed and no buffalo appeared save one moribund, blind brown bull, the evenings became longer, more dangerous. Already it was the Moon of Water Freezing when darkness settled early. There was nothing sociable about Boggs's drinking now. The stories were used up. He simply planted his feet, tilted back his head, and sucked the liquor down in long, steady draughts. When Yellow Bird asked him why he drank, Boggs replied, "There's this rock inside me. Right here," and he pointed to his chest. "I'm trying to melt it down, if you don't mind." That was all right, but it had been a mistake to interrupt his self-absorption, for now Boggs began a discourse on Indians.

"Greasy, grimy, greedy, and gassy, the four G's, that's what Indians are. Stubborn as mules, and just about as ambitious. Good for nothing but mule's work. Not that I'm speaking of you, old man, you fair-haired beauty. There's a white man up your family tree somewhere. Bet your mom was a real looker, eh?"

Yellow Bird bit down, tasting blood in his saliva. It was not his own blood, but Boggs's, and he feared his sudden impulse to destroy the man. His long restraint was beginning to break down. More than anything he wanted to strike at that red face with its lopsided grin. In his mind he was searching for a place to lodge his knife when Boggs said, "Does it ever hurt?"

"What?" Yellow Bird was caught by surprise. Had his thoughts been discovered?

"That old wound of yours. Gunshot? Did a white or a red man do it? Maybe it's having all that white blood that makes you such a piss poor guide. Half-breed never can track like a full-blood. Might have done better on my own. Sometimes I think you're not trying very hard. Or maybe you're trying too damned hard, running me round in circles, thinking you can hoodwink old B.B. Can't. Can't outthink me. Sure can't out- drink me, neither." He lifted the bottle, held it poised slant- wise, sucked the amber lightning into his gullet. "Come on, Yellow Bird. If you're the better man, prove it." He pushed the bottle at Yellow Bird. "Drink up with a pal."

From the beginning Yellow Bird had known that they were enemies, but now for the first time he sensed that Boggs also knew. He took the bottle, which otherwise would have been shoved neck first between his teeth, and drank. As long as he kept swallowing, there was no fire and no taste. Afterward came the hot skewering. It was cheap whiskey, full of tobacco juice and pepper—rotgut for the Indian trade. Beads of sweat burst out on Yellow Bird's forehead, big as birdshot pellets.

"You, too, woman." Boggs made Deer Walking take a tin cup, made her pour it full. Her hands trembled so that the liquor spilled as the bottle chattered against the tin. "Damn it, get hold of yourself," he told her in a fierce whisper.

"Damn you," she replied in English. Her voice was hard and brittle as ice as she slowly poured the whiskey out onto the ground. "I'm not my father. I'm not your woman," she added in the tongue of her people.

Boggs watched the provocative beauty of her gesture, and his ears seemed to move back in fury. "By God!" he said. "By God, I'll knock every one of your crooked teeth out." His hands knotted into fists as he tried to get up, but the whiskey grabbed him by the seat of the pants. "That's a promise, woman, soon as I make up my mind to it."

Boggs had threatened before. There'd been worse times, but taken all together, the balance was finally ready to shift. Yellow Bird sensed it, and he knew that Deer Walking felt it, too. Regardless of the white buffalo, it was time to clear out. When Boggs was finally snoring in the wagon, a few hasty words were enough for the details. They'd leave him the wagon and the mules, but they would take the two horses so that he would not follow with his long-range rifle.

They were saddling the horses when Boggs suddenly banged out of the wagon. He took the long step down as though it were a short one, and the fall seemed to sober him. He heaved himself to his feet. "Hey, where you two going? Answer me, you Indian bitch!" With teeth wet and slobbery as a dog's, he showered them with spittle in his rage. Seizing his horse's nose rope in one hand, he tried at the same time to hit Deer Walking in the eye. The vagrant blow carried the rest of him along with it, and he fell again, still clutching the leads. Under his body was the belted pistol, and he fumbled for it.

Yellow Bird pulled his pony free, yanked Deer Walking to her feet, and ran. Perhaps it was his white blood that sent him crashing through torn patches while the girl ran lightly, as unobstructed as a hovering bird. Then the first shot rang out. They ran faster, reaching for darkness, but they could not outrun Boggs's terrible claim. More shots were flung after them. Deer Walking began to lag. He tried to support her, but she grew heavy on his arm.

"You can ride," he urged her. "Hurry, get on my pony."

"I can go no farther," she murmured. "This is death." Only then did he feel the warm dampness spreading across the back of her dress. In the end he carried her, painfully, her weight growing as her body lost blood. At a point where the campfire was one with the distant stars, Yellow Bird stopped and gently set her down. She shaped a smile for him, and died without another word.

He had outlived too many deaths. This one he could not bear. Blind fury sent him raging back to find the bullet that had missed him. His unfeeling feet were torn by stones, his legs ripped by thorns. A tree trunk spun him down, but he kept going, scrabbling on all fours until he was running again. He stood at last in the circle of firelight, an unmoving target as Boggs took slow aim and missed, steadied his whiskeyed arm with the other hand, and missed again. Four shots went wild, and then the fifth threw up a spray of stone chips. With them came pain, calling his body to life. His body did not want to die, and Yellow Bird ducked away before the sixth shot could catch him. His body ran in shameless panic, as detached from his mind as a runaway horse. Hidden again, Yellow Bird called himself a coward before the Gods. Let them crush him like a worm. But as he lay there, breathing agonized gulps of air, he knew his legs were more right than he. There was no good in dying while Boggs had warm blood in his body.

Death for death. When he returned it would be as a warrior. He searched for and finally found his pony, quietly cropping grass not far from where Yellow Bird had left him. He shook dirt from a gopher's hole upon the pony, so that like the gopher it might have the wisdom of concealment. He mounted, but was weaponless; even his bow had been left in camp. Only by surprise could he kill Boggs. The camp was still as he approached the second time. The fire was out, not even smoldering. Only the clicking of autumn's last crickets and the shrill sawing of cicadas broke the silence. Dismounting, he crept forward. One quick burst would carry him across the clear ground to the wagon. He was up on his haunches, a runner awaiting the signal, when Boggs emerged, this time with his long-range rifle in his hands. "You damned white buffalo!" he bellowed. "Damn buffalo!" He let the gun off at the sky, and the blast of it reverberated like rolling thunder. Another shot whistled past Yellow Bird. He felt the heat of it and was afraid.

At the first shot his pony had stampeded into the dark, and for the second time Yellow Bird fled on foot. He felt his way through the tall rustling grass until he came again to the tree under which Deer Walking lay. He called to her to arise, to make a lie of it. How could one stray bullet have cut her down when so many deliberately aimed had passed him by? He knelt for a long time beside her, full of grief and weariness and shame. Lightning had begun to flicker, and he became aware of a vast ghost cloud towering high above him. The wind came suddenly, flattening the grass. Faint and far-off he heard those voices which spoke to him always in riddles. Ready for the warpath, they were flinging out their fire arrows. He called upon them to help him. "O Grandfathers, behold me. You who know the dark giant in his power, behold me, Yellow Bird. Hear my prayers and give me strength. Tell me what I must do." And though he did not understand them, the voices gave him comfort; they were his friends, his family. Now their louder mutterings seemed to reply, "It is time. Behold."

The lightning traveled down cloudy mountains and painted things to come, the red road, the sacred tree bursting into bloom, while the voices spoke more and more forcefully of dark command and prophecy. Nearer now, a bolt tore through the air. The earth, Deer Walking's face glowed incandescent and then vanished into blackness. On the rising wind he heard other voices, the cries of crows and coyotes, of buffalo and bear, shouts of the dead and the not yet born, reviling him, telling him that he had failed, that he had strayed from his life's purpose, that now it was time to act.

With a fearful splitting sound, a rush of rending light nearly blinded him, but in its glare he saw Crazy Horse, immense, eyes blazing, reach down to touch him, and that touch burned and flung him to the shaken earth. He saw the tree under which he had sheltered split and fall, squealing like a stricken beast. Blue flames licked along its wounded trunk. Fire sprang up at his feet, rising through the dry seed tops of the bluestem and bunch grass. The grandfathers had told Yellow Bird what to do. With a wild laugh, he made a twisted brand of dry grass and dragged flames out into a long advancing crescent. A jack rabbit caught fire and bounded away, laying a wide trail of flame. Yellow Bird gazed at his handiwork, a half mile of spreading cremation, moving east toward Boggs's wagon, toward the land of the white man. He was a wildfire himself, ready to brush aside all obstacles. Overhead the thunder voices cheered him on, urged on his crackling demon army. His lungs burned from shouting aloud. It was the cry of the eagle set free.

The wind-driven fire had no wish to stop. It rolled on through the grass and scrub until it glowed like dawn along the eastern sky. Something ignited in a towering plume of fire. The wagon? Yellow Bird thought he heard a cry, sucked from the fire's steady roar. Where the flames had passed, red spots glittered like fox eyes in the dark.

Finally the rain came, warm for autumn, and heavy. The sky seemed to set hands upon him, telling him that all was well, to lie down, to rest. These things he did, waking with a bitter mouth and the sound of a bird cracking seeds in the stillness. A smell of burning hung in the air. The fire must have outrun the rain, for as far as he could see in the east the earth was blackened and smoldering. But in all that waste, only one thing mattered to Yellow Bird, and he set out through the charred debris to make sure.

So much had changed he had trouble finding the camp. The metal rim of one of the wagon's wheels signaled to him, then the fallen skeleton of the wagon itself. Poking through its ruined contents, he probed at a charred blanket with a stick and saw what he thought to be a protruding wrist and hand, cracked, shiny, and black. Boggs. A bird mocked him in its flight, three high notes. He thrust at the hand and it broke into brittle fragments, showing itself to be no hand at all, but wood. Then Yellow Bird tore at the rubble, hurling it, kicking it about, until he himself was charcoaled from head to foot. There was no sign of Boggs.

Later, when he composed himself and searched the wider desolation, he found not a clue. Boggs, his arrows, his pony, all were gone. Yellow Bird was alone in a charred waste with Deer Walking. In his despair, he would have shot the white buffalo and made of its hide a funeral robe for her, but he had only a piece of scorched canvas to wrap her in. This he did, and then with his bare hands he dug her grave. He dug deep, until the calluses were torn from his palms and his fingers were raw. His blood mixed with hers in that unmarked grave. For a day and a night he lingered. Then with a cry, less like a human voice than the howl of a wolf in the lonely night, he turned and walked away, slowly at first, his head down, then faster. As he went, Yellow Bird made a pledge to the sky. He would find Boggs again. He would find him if he failed in everything else. He would find him and have his revenge or die.

VII

The Indian Christ

Yellow Bird returned to the reservation without Deer Walking, without seeing the white buffalo, without revenge. His people, too, were without hope in the Freezing Moon of that year which the white man called 1888. Strangely, he was not moved by their despair, for he had seen Crazy Horse in the lightning flash, and nothing really spoke to him in the physical world except as an echo of the visions he had seen. However detached he had felt since that storm, it had infused in him a new power and deftness in medicine. Somehow, through his hands, power could be transmitted from the storm, as the white man's singing wires carried sparks and messages. This gift was never more needed. There was whooping cough on the reservation, worse than in years past because of the log cabins in which so many now lived: square boxes with none of the earth's healing power, which always worked in circles.

During that winter he visited many lodges where children lay wrapped in their blankets and death already danced outside. Some died under his hands without ever feeling the lightning in his fingertips. Others he knew to be cured as he felt the power surging through him, as he put his lips to their racked bodies and blew through them the cleansing storm-wind. Then he knelt with tears in his eyes and thanked the Powers for their help. Yellow Bird relied on few charms and did not paint himself, though before each call he rubbed dirt upon himself to admit to the Powers that he was helpless without their assistance. For the thunders whose rain brought renewal, he sometimes beat upon a drum. Then it was as though the storm raged inside him, but he never gave way to frenzy. He exercised his gift with deliberate calculation.

Among his patients was Big Foot once again. He was tall and cadaverous, his long legs nearly touching the ground on either side of his pony as he rode, coughing and spitting, to Yellow Bird's lodge. For a long time he could not speak for coughing. Finally he apologetically wiped his mouth with the sleeve of his doeskin hunting shirt, where a patch was dark with old blood. Because Big Foot said he was bad only in winter, Yellow Bird blew dried flower petals in his face. He called on the Powers of the south, of summer and the sun, to take care of the old chief, and when Big Foot rode away he did not cough.

Though the Powers seemed to smile upon his medicine, Yellow Bird cured only individuals. He could do nothing for his people as a whole; their spirit seemed sick beyond curing or prayer. "O Great Spirit, you have fashioned the world. You made it good. You made the red road and the black. You who have put the heat in the sun and power in the storm, to you I send my voice for help." Until the spring no sign was given, but then the thunders muttered again in the west.

Because their voices still confused him, and because the storm itself was contrary, bringing destruction as well as the grass-growing rain, Yellow Bird dressed as a heyoka, a sacred fool, so that he might seem funny and serious at the same time. With black lightning streaks painted upon his body, he began his vision dance by walking backward in the manner of a contrary. He made a show of testing a mud puddle for depth with his bow, which he laid flat, pretending it was as deep as the bow's length so that he might safely dive in and swim. This he attempted to do while the people and the thunder voices in the west laughed approval. Finally, while lightning brightened the horizon, he sacrificed a dog, quickly and bloodlessly as the lightning bolt. The washed body he offered to the thunder beings, and their acknowledgment shook the ground. Many of those who watched his performance ran for shelter as the wind gathered itself, as lightning devoured a tall pine just outside the camp circle. Until the storm passed, Yellow Bird danced his vision of the red road that was lost and the sacred tree that would not blossom, and it was after this dance that the news first arrived with a drenched and shivering party of Arapaho hunters. They had taken shelter in a culvert and been swept away and nearly drowned by a flash flood, and they brought the news of one who dwelt beyond the shining mountains.

It was said that the Great Spirit's son, whom the white men called Messiah and had nailed to a tree, had come again among the Indians. If they treated him well and loved him, he would lift up the weary earth and make it as it had been before the white man. Then the ancestors would return to life, and Indians would travel upon the earth as they wished, riding fine ponies among herds of buffalo without ending. This Wanekia, this one who made life, lived in the land of the fish-eaters, it was said, between the last great mountains and the sea. There was no human tongue he did not understand and he would speak to all men. Already Utes, Snakes, and Bannocks had visited, and returned in wonder.

There was talk of this at Standing Rock. Some said it was foolish chatter, but others yearned to believe. A few wanted to follow the western star that was said to burn above the valley where the Messiah lived. Among these were Good Thunder, who conversed with the storm as did Yellow Bird, and Cloud Horse. Since the government agent would refuse them permission for such a journey, no permission was asked. When the chosen few gathered to depart, Yellow Bird was among them. He would have gone alone if necessary, for in the darkness in which his people trod the black road to extinction, the rumors came as a last and dazzling hope that the red road might be found to lead them to the sacred tree. Perhaps now the tree would bloom once more.

The party set out in the Moon of the Bull Buffalo's Rutting, riding their ponies to the Fort Hall reservation. There the Shoshoni and Bannock danced in the new way, calling it a dance for the ghosts of their ancestors who would return. From Fort Hall they would take the train. Many would ride the rails, and those who had passes, as Yellow Bird had from Chief Big Foot, would sit inside the cars. The station where they waited smelled of dead cigars and sweat. It was plastered with old posters, beauties of the stage with their waists drawn in and their bosoms popping out, mustachioed acrobats swinging from high bars. All the posters were flyblown, cobwebbed, and splattered with tobacco juice.

When the westbound train puffed in two hours later, the passengers stampeded into the station to eat black salty ham, and biscuits that looked as hard as case shot, off grimy checked tablecloths. A small man with stringy thin hair and a green eyeshade looked over Yellow Bird's pass suspiciously, then reluctantly told him to board the train. He chose a coach seat next to an empty coal stove and bought an overpriced hardboiled egg from the boy who passed through the car aisles with magazines and cigars. The egg was slippery, but Yellow Bird expected little else for the next two days, so he chewed it down. With closed eyes he waited as though the hour that passed was only an instant in his eternity. Finally the conductor waved his arm and the whistle sucked the station restaurant empty. Slowly they jolted west into the open furnace of the late afternoon.

Through nameless tank and prairie dog towns the train chased the lowering sun. Morning found the role reversed. Passengers were loaded at Ogden, among them a large party from Salt Lake City. Some of these Mormons wore white robes, and they talked about the Indian Messiah as if they too believed. Their founding father had been told by a heavenly voice that, should he live to be eighty-five years old, he would see the face of the Son of Man. Joseph Smith was long departed, but now those years had run. Yellow Bird, though he sat with his chin down and his eyes closed as if in sleep, heard all this and was astounded. He was amazed, too, to hear that his people were descended from the lost tribes of Israel. Surely the world was stirred by great events. Drugged with this thought and the heat of the closed car, Yellow Bird was nearly asleep when a large man with a cheerful pudding face entered the car. His black robes suggested some divine association even before he revealed the tarnished cross that hung from his belt.

He sat down facing Yellow Bird, his hands clasped, his face thrust slightly forward. "My poor soul," he murmured, making a vague motion with his right hand that seemed to combine wiping his brow with scattering holy water. He spoke now in a tongue that Yellow Bird thought he recognized as the language he had heard in New York at the white man's holy place. As the pronouncement was aimed in Yellow Bird's general direction, he said, "I speak only English."

"English?" the holy man replied. "How nice. Traveling to see the world? Relatives?"

"To see God," Yellow Bird told him.

"Indeed," came the response. "God is my business, too. I have come west to teach His Indian children to love Jesus." With this he took a black book from his wide sleeve and seemed for a time to find refuge in it, but before Yellow Bird could drift off again he produced a picture card that evidently had served as a book marker. The subject matter filled Yellow Bird with horror, for though he had seen it before, it had never been so bloodily portrayed. He had seen it not only in the books of the Black Robes but also in New York and in London, where white men prayed to the one they had murdered, the one they called the Messiah. To discover more, he decided to appear more ignorant than he really was.

"Him bad man to be punished that way."

The holy man laughed out loud, tore off his spectacles, exhaled on the glass, rubbed them on his robe, and put them back on again. "Appearances can be wrong. He is a very good and great man. There is none greater."

"Him not dead?" asked Yellow Bird. Indeed, it was a marvel that anyone could survive such torture, so many wounds. Surely scars would remain. He would look for them when he met the Messiah.

"No, of course not. He lives forever. He is my God and yours. One day He will return to us all."

"To punish the white man for nailing him up on sticks?"

"No, my son. To love and redeem us all, red and white."

"He has returned already," Yellow Bird explained, sur-

[168]

rendering his role of ignorant heathen. "I shall soon visit him."

"Where did you get such a remarkable idea?" asked the holy man. Yellow Bird mentioned the stories he had heard. "My son, you are better off disregarding such tales. Prophecies are sown through history like seed." Yellow Bird resented being called son. The other was not his father—more likely, in fact, an enemy than a friend. Perhaps the man sensed this resistance, for he added, "It is up to those who wear the black robe to announce His coming."

"He has come."

"Yes, and been crucified, dead, and buried."

"He has come again," Yellow Bird insisted.

"He will come again, but not yet."

"He has not come for you," Yellow Bird explained patiently. "You nailed him up. You would nail him up again."

"Now, now, my boy, no need to be abusive. But to answer your question, He will come in His own good time to all men. He will bring in a great new age."

"Will he bring his woman?" Yellow Bird asked, examining the other side of the card, which showed a female figure wrapped in a blue trade blanket, her eyes cast dotingly upon a baby in her arms.

"That is Mary, His mother."

"You lie," Yellow Bird insisted. "The earth is his mother."

"Lie?" The holy man appeared to be in pain. "No, no, my son, I do not lie. This is His mother, the holy Virgin Mary. His father is God Almighty, who is everywhere and in all things. He is in the little spiderwebs that come at dawn and in the long shadows of the night. God the Father is in the pine forest and on the mountaintop and in the trout swimming deep in the lake. He is in the tiny centipede and in the great buffalo. He is inside the white man and He is inside you. Always, He sees everything. You cannot hide from Him in a cave, you cannot hide from Him in the dark or under your blankets. Day and night He watches everything we do."

"I do not like this peeping god of yours. If he were on our reservation, the police would arrest him," Yellow Bird observed.

"You were placed here to try my faith," the holy man answered. When he summarily retired behind the wall of his black book, Yellow Bird still held the painted card with the pictures of the poor-devil white man hung up by nails and of his blanketed mother. Perhaps the new baby on her lap would help her forget the suffering of her other son. These whites, he thought. If they weren't mad, then he had never been sane. At the same time, he knew their god had great power. He must be brother to the Great Spirit, and if one were to judge by results, a big brother. He would keep the picture card, for it was a strange thing and must contain strong magic.

By this time the train was rocking up a rough roadbed into high country where dark pine forests were streaked with falling streams. Here and there were high, bare cliffs; far off, the mountains gleamed, rank on rank, translucent against the sky.

The Messiah lived among the Paiute people in the Mason Valley, a land of ancient upheaval where the Sierras rose high on either side. They were black volcanic escarpments, darkly forested and crowned with snow. The valley soil, watered by the Walker River, supported many ranches, and the Paiute, the Messiah among them, worked for the white man.

Not knowing how to proceed from the weatherbeaten clapboard depot, Yellow Bird and his companions sought a guide.

They found one propped against the station wall, a dusty old Paiute with bags under his rheumy eyes.

Yellow Bird tapped him with one foot to make sure he was alive.

The old man took hold of his ankle. "Heap sonabitch," he said in English.

"What's your name?" Yellow Bird asked in the same language.

"Charley Sheep," he replied. "I look after sheep."

"We want a guide."

"You like beautiful girl to bring moon and stars into your lodge?"

"Only a guide to Wovoka, the Messiah."

"The Dreamer," he sighed, and Yellow Bird's nostrils received a blast of cheap whiskey and old age. "Give me minne wakan and I will go."

"No whiskey. Food. Get up." Yellow Bird pulled Charley Sheep to his feet and the old man clutched his wrist.

"Give me drink and I will take you. A man cannot travel empty." He had given away his tomahawk and his moccasins to the people passing on the trains. Everything had been traded for firewater. Yellow Bird now offered him hardtack, but with the surprising grace of a conjurer, Charley Sheep produced a rusty tin cup full of red pepper, tobacco juice, and whiskey. He fixed Yellow Bird with a feverish eye, then upended the cup and gulped the contents down.

"Now eat. Here. Cheese."

"Red man can eat. He can drink whiskey. Can't do both. Whiskey is like God. I look at stars, I want whiskey. I see sun, I want whiskey." He coughed, then made a gluey, rippling sound, which Yellow Bird realized was a kind of laugh. He

fumbled finally with the cheese and hardtack, which were
stuck to a bit of paper, managed to fold the three together in
a sandwich and munched them down absently while extolling
the virtues of minne wakan, his holy water: the way to truth,
paradise in a bottle.

Though Charley Sheep was an unpromising bit of humanity,
Yellow Bird wasn't going to let his investment slide back onto
the depot's floor. Some night soon he would fall down forever,
lost between the white man's Lord God of Hosts, and his own
wizened deity. Then frost would form over him, but not now.
Outside, in the clawing mountain cold, Charley Sheep seemed
to collect himself. By the time they had reached the railroad
bridge, he was able to walk the rail without stumbling into
the river.

The trail led along the mountain fringe through muffling,
gloomy pines high above ranch and pasture. It was well and
freshly worn. It was followed by many tribes: Cheyenne and
Arapaho and Nez Percé as well as the Ree, those small, sooty
men who had always been sworn enemies of the Sioux. All were
brothers now, all full of talk, a babble of tongues that seemed
oddly intelligible to all. All spoke of the Messiah. Many called
him "Our Father," or Wovoka. Others called him Jack Wilson
or Big Rumbling Belly. It was said he named himself Cutter,
since he had been a carpenter cutting wood when he had heard
a great noise in the sky. As the sun had been extinguished, he
had fallen dead on the spot and been lifted up to heaven. He
and the sun had been reborn together. Ever since, he could
make animals speak, could travel as a cloud, and could com-
municate with the Great Spirit of the universe. The Spirit
had told him that paradise was to come, and that the dead
would live again with their relatives.

[172]

Such matters were being discussed as Yellow Bird waited outside Wovoka's lodge, where the Messiah reportedly lay beneath a blanket, singing to himself of worlds to come. Only on the second day, toward evening, did the prophet reveal himself. Then he emerged smiling from his lodge, not as though dozens of Indians from many tribes had been noisily awaiting him, but as a hunter steps outside, to find the weather good. Wovoka was a tall man, Yellow Bird judged, and heavy-set. On his head was a white, broad-brimmed hat, and he wore a white man's shirt as well—white, with symbols of the sun and moon upon it. His wide, friendly face was neither as dark as an Indian's nor as light as a white man's. His hair was cut square below his ears in Paiute fashion, and an eagle feather dangled from one elbow. Remembering the picture card of the crucifixion, Yellow Bird looked at Wovoka's hard-muscled hands for scars. He saw one on the man's wrist and another on his face. Surely this was the true Messiah.

Wovoka moved out under the cottonwood trees where the campfires glowed dully. He stood on a tanned deerskin and made a signal to a companion. As Yellow Bird watched in horror, the other raised a sawed-off shotgun and fired. Buckshot fell from the Messiah's cotton shirt and scattered harmlessly at his feet. Only then, with the smell of powder upon him, did Wovoka return to the ring of beaten earth. He stood in the firelight, bowing his head in prayer. Looking up at last, he said, "My children, I have sent for you and I am glad you have come. I want you to listen while I tell you about your relatives who are gone but who will return. I will teach you how to dance." Most of this Yellow Bird comprehended, though many of the strong, rolling words, some in English, others in some Indian dialect, were beyond his ken. It was as though

Wovoka spoke in pictures, in music that felt as searing to Yellow Bird's soul as flung sparks.

"When the sun died," Wovoka was saying, "I went up to heaven and saw the Great Spirit and all the ancestors who died long ago. The Great Spirit told me to return and tell the People that they must be good and love one another. There must be no more fighting, no more stealing, no more lying. You must be kind to the animals that serve you, the horse and the dog. The red man and the white man must live as brothers. And then, when the People are worthy, there will come a day in spring when there will be no more sickness. Your ancestors will return and all men will be young forever."

Those who had gathered about Wovoka listened intently, some in fear, some in doubt. Many wrote the Messiah's message down in crude English, but Yellow Bird had come expecting a bolt of lightning. He had envisioned a wolf, and saw only a white dove. It would take more than a speech to win him over. Later, in the darkness of Wovoka's lodge, the Messiah sat behind a small fire. Moths fluttered around his head. He held his white hat on his knees and invited the visitors, one by one, to gaze inside it. Some looked into the crown of the hat and shook their heads; others turned away quickly as though their eyes had been scalded. Yellow Bird peered down and saw nothing at first but the hat, and shadows. Then, like something rising through clear, still water, he saw a world reflected, green and full of game. Familiar faces were there, softened by the years. His mother raised her hand and beckoned. The moment was beyond explaining. He had not anticipated paradise in a white felt hat; now he lived in it. He felt an endless procession of people sweep around him, restless, wind-borne, unable to catch hold of anything solid. As Yellow

Bird gazed deeper, he seemed to behold in the distance an intense light. It approached rapidly, becoming a man clad in shining white. "Crazy Horse," he exclaimed, his eyes dazzled. Yellow Bird drew away, shutting his vision-haunted eyes, and so it happened that he came to believe. He had found the way at last. His feet would not stray again from the path, his eyes would not close to the vision.

When all who wished to do so had examined the hat, Wovoka rose and said, "Now, my children, it is time to make ready for the dancing in a circle, for that is the way we give thanks for what will come." The dancing would go on for four consecutive nights.

With their fingers linked, men and women moved together in a huge, slow, leg-dragging circle. The step was strange to Yellow Bird. It was like sliding out a tentative foot to test ice for its thinness. They all stumbled uncertainly at first, then gained confidence and were no longer separate people but one great living chain, the hoop of life renewing itself, turning inexorably like the sun and moon, like the seasons, driven by the grave, slow beat of a drum. The pace kept up throughout the night. Feet and hands grew numb, seemed to vanish altogether. Yellow Bird felt himself a detached spirit, cocooned in drowsiness and yet uplifted, seeing the arc of faces like spheres of copper hung in the fire glow.

> *Our father has come,*
> *Our father has come,*
> *The earth has come,*
> *The earth has come.*

They sang it over and over, while a huge, resonant drum beat as though it were the earth's heart. It beat in Yellow

Bird's head, beat to match his own heart until dawn broke the weary circle. The dancers were suddenly exuberant, running, shedding their clothes, plunging into the icy stream. The cold shot deep as fire, numbed all sensation, and Yellow Bird remembered a day long past on the Greasy Grass and felt somehow that he had come full circle.

Throughout the days of talk and the nights of dancing, new pilgrims arrived. Most of them were old. All were instructed with the message of peace and love, versed in the dance of the ghosts of the ancestors, and sent back to their own people. Yellow Bird could not bear to turn away at once, though hard winter was coming and his friends could no longer wait. When he finally departed, alone, he felt the Messiah fly above him, teaching him the sacred songs for the dance all the way to the train depot.

There he waited overnight with Charley Sheep gurgling beside him. It was so cold they had to roll up in the abandoned "prairie monitor," an underground fortress designed to resist sudden attack. The wind whistled through the gun slits, whispering messages, telling him to hurry, to spread the gospel of Wovoka and Crazy Horse. Snow followed him on the trip back. It held him up twice in the mountains, and delayed the train again before he reached Fort Hall. Finally, as the sun rolled up over the endless white expanse, Yellow Bird mounted his pony and headed east, alone.

On the second day out, Yellow Bird saw a buffalo mired in a deep snow pocket. If I don't eat you, the wolves will, he told it before spilling out its life with one shot behind the ear. He ate strips of its flesh raw for that rich taste he had almost forgotten. This buffalo was a sign, he told himself, and he turned in the direction of Wovoka's home to thank the Messiah for remembering him. After he had done this, he seemed to see the slain buffalo come to life again, lift its head, then gather its legs beneath its body, shift its weight forward, and move off, tail switching.

That night he holed up at the base of a fir tree. It was bitterly cold. He managed to set a small, smoky fire, and toward dawn he slept. He dreamed of many buffalo milling around him in a slow, dragging circle, and later he dreamed of Crazy Horse. The warrior chief was dressed in glowing white again, and he was hung upon a cross. Bluecoat soldiers came and fired their guns at him, but the bullets fell harmlessly away. Then Crazy Horse pulled his nailed hands away from the wood. He stepped down, and the bluecoats were afraid. They dropped their guns and vanished like smoke on the wind.

When Yellow Bird awoke, it was as though he had not dreamed, for he saw many hoofprints on the frozen ground. Where the ground was blown clear of snow, buffalo grazed. With such good omens, when he was so certain of his powers, it was strange that he should feel such sadness in his heart.

Wafer-thin clouds were melting under the devouring sun as he rode on. Soon he had left the grazing buffalo behind, but in the eastern sky soared buzzards, lifting toward the clouds. Death was there, and he rode toward it, seeing finally snow-laden scrub, a large boulder, a tethered horse, and traces of frozen blood. A second inspection told him the great stone was something else, with head, body, and frozen limbs. It was a buffalo, and from its belly protruded a human hand.

"Hey, you! Help me out!" emerged a muffled voice.

A hunter had taken night refuge from the cold in the warm carcass of his kill, and now the hide had frozen hard as iron about him. Men had died that way. The midday sun would thaw this carcass out. Already the shadow of the bushes had nearly passed. Again the hand waved at him. He waved back, approaching near enough to see eyes, whiskers, cheeks burned red as raw meat. The sight struck him like the hot touch of an arrow. Billy Boggs!

"Stranger, you got an ax?"

Remembering Boggs's pistol, Yellow Bird stepped to the side. Already the sun had placed a golden finger on the frosty hide. Soon there would be no need for an ax. He had none, in any case, and for his purpose a coiled rope would do. This Yellow Bird secured to the buffalo's horns, and in so doing dusted away the film of snow and frost. The curly hair was white. White! His hands played over the hide. White. All white. Again the voice called to him: "Stranger, do you have a bite of food? There's some in my pack. Stranger?" The line was tight, the sun full on the carcass when Yellow Bird urged his pony ahead. Together they moved the huge cadaver, with its contents silent at such mysterious activity. They went slowly at first, but faster as the slope and the momentum increased until the remains came to rest in a dry watercourse. Deeply shadowed and with a subterranean cold, it would not be visited by the sun's warmth until summer.

Yellow Bird undid the rope, and coiled it. He mounted his pony, urging him back up the grade. As the pony's mane flowed golden in the sunlight, a cry rose behind them, a cry of realization and despair. Before departing, Yellow Bird examined Boggs's camp. He found some dried meat, long and thin like the sausage he'd had in London. He chewed some of it and washed it down with snow water. The pack further disclosed a small bag of coins. He took it, along with the pistol

[178]

with *BB* cut into the grip. Then, with Boggs's horse roped behind his own, he headed east again. As he passed the watercourse, a fearful inhuman scream, like a tormented bugle
sounding the last charge, tried to catch hold of him. It seemed
to go on and on as he rode, a silver thread of sound cast in
great loops until he knew no human, red or white, could cry
out so long.

The words of the Messiah had already reached the reservation before Yellow Bird returned to add to them, but he had
dreams and visions of buffalo and of Crazy Horse turning back
the soldiers' bullets. The Big Bellies saw Yellow Bird winter-
lean with the ghost of death in him. They heard him out and
their pipes died as they listened. He showed them a shirt he
had made. It was white, painted with buffalo horns, the moon,
the stars, and the red disk of the rising sun. An eagle feather
was sewn to each fringed sleeve. "No white man's bullet will
pass through it," he assured them, and many believed him and
made shirts of their own, calling them ghost shirts. One young
brave fired at his companion and laid him writhing in the grass
before they could be made to understand that the magic cloth
was proof only against the white man's bullets.

"Is it a war shirt, then?" old Big Foot asked him. His cough
had come again, and he wished nothing to do with fighting.

"No, it is a shirt for dancing," Yellow Bird told him. "It
will help the People toward the great day. Already the spirit
host waits in the west beyond the horizon. They wait only
for their great leader, Crazy Horse, to raise his hand." They
must put on the holy shirts and dance and, dancing, change
the earth. They must gather around the sacred tree and make
it sprout. Then the earth would shiver and the floods would
come, lifting up all who believed. Those who did not believe

would become small and hard and be burned on the lodge fires. The white men would be cast out and down into the mud. A great demon with huge cracking knee joints would pull them down, leaving only the People on the earth. Then the dead ancestors would return. They would be forever young. The blind would see again, and all would see boundless prairies full of game. It would all come with the spring, one year away, if they believed, and danced, and made the withered tree flower again.

For the coming dance, a pine tree, painted red and decked with eagle feathers and buffalo horns, was erected in the dance circle. Many braves fasted in preparation and purified themselves in the sweat lodge. No metal or weapons were allowed in the dance. By now many had fashioned ghost shirts. The women wore robes with flowing sleeves decorated with birds and beasts, and they outnumbered the men. Old criers went out toward sundown to announce the dance. The first few people joined hands and began to move from right to left, following the sun around the withered tree and the huddle of ill and dying at its base. "Heal us, Father, give us back our arrows," they implored. Slowly the dancing circle enlarged. Yellow Bird began a song that the Messiah had taught him. Other voices joined him.

> *You shall see your grandfather,*
> *The father says so.*
> *You shall see your kindred,*
> *The father says so.*

The chant went on and on, pleading, demanding, as the dancers revolved, following a deepening path that led nowhere. Yellow Bird felt that he danced above the ground. Faces, figures revolved. The turning tree seemed to flower with an endless variety of colored fruits. "It lives!" he shouted aloud, and voices of the living and the dead seemed to echo him. "The tree lives!" A woman ahead of him tottered out of line. She staggered drunkenly, her eyes glazed, with only the milky whites showing. Yellow Bird revolved about her, shaking his medicine stick until she fell, quivering, pawing the air. Others collapsed and were left on the ground.

Later, when they awoke, some went away silently bewildered, and a few were sick, while others told of seeing their warrior dead. One man found a beaded trinket, which he said had belonged to a relative who had died long ago. Another produced buffalo tail meat, saying he had seen great herds. All the while the droning dance went on, as people called out their sorrow and hope under a starlit haze of dust. In the sky Yellow Bird saw warriors riding, a trample of ghost riders spilling down the clouds, their shields of old striped in many colors, their lances bright. "They come! See them!" he screamed, while something behind the clouds, beyond the sky, something terrible, seemed silently to smile.

VIII

Murder and the Performing Horse

Yellow Bird saw green pastures to come, all the greener for the dryness of the emerging summer and of the summer before. The agency chiefs, Gall, John Grass, and Crow King, had signed away half of what remained of the Indian land. Only Sitting Bull had made an outcry, saying, "Indians? There are no Indians left but me." He had put a curse upon the sky so that no rain would come, so that the crops of the new white pioneers would fail along with the Indian corn. It was a strong curse, for Shell King, who had tried to undo it, had been struck dead by dry lightning.

At dawn no clouds piled above the Black Hills. Day after day the sun glared down and at night the stars were hard as ice. Streams ceased to run. The stream beds turned to clay. The clay split, became dust, and blew in the air. Grasshoppers flung themselves out of the brassy sky to devour the spring corn, which had begun to dry and wilt. The People trekked back and forth to the agencies with wagons and ration sacks, and their children's bellies were blown up with emptiness. Then from Washington came word that the rations were to be cut because a hungry Indian was supposed to make a more dedicated farmer. Some stayed at the agencies, demanding food. Others wandered home to find that birds and wild animals had eaten what was left of their crops.

The white man's diseases, whooping cough and measles, the hunger, the dying, the vanishment of their sacred lands, all this piling up of evils broke down confidence in the old way of life. More ghost shirts appeared, and people danced who would not dance at first. By autumn the rain had still not come. Reluctant clouds climbed the western sky to be chased away by the bitter dusty wind. The only hope was the Messiah, and the change that would come in the spring. At the Cheyenne River reserve, old Big Foot, whose cough was bad, put faith in Yellow Bird, and the people danced each night.

There had been four periods in Yellow Bird's life, and this was the best. First there had been the time of innocence, of not knowing, when he had been an Indian in an Indian world. Next had come the time of awareness, when he had lost the people he loved. This was a time of sorrow and hatred. There had followed a time of confusion and years of searching and the first beginnings of hope. Now the search was over, the hope resolved. This was his time of knowing, and he could look confidently at the sky, which seemed to smile upon his prospects.

The only flaw was Sitting Bull. At his Standing Rock camp, there was ghost dancing led by Kicking Bear and Bull Ghost, but Sitting Bull himself kept apart and spoke nothing of the Messiah. Troubled by this lack of interest, Yellow Bird determined to talk with the man whose presence had always stilled his tongue. In the Moon of Water Freezing he went to Sitting Bull's cabin. That the great chief lived in a white man's house, piled high with trunks, sewing machines, rocking chairs, a brass bed, that he rode a white man's circus horse distressed Yellow Bird.

The chief, despite his accumulation of goods, seemed to have changed little. When Yellow Bird arrived, he was glaring into a mirror and picking out whiskers with a bone tweezer. He must have known Yellow Bird was there, but he did not at once look up from his task. Finally he stood, a little stiffer, a little more rigid of muscle as well as of pride. "Yellow Bird, grandson," he said and held out both hands, his square face glowing. "I have heard much of you."

"You live well, Grandfather," Yellow Bird replied.

"Yes, I live well enough."

"Like a white man."

"In some things. The white men are not fools, and there are some among them who would help us. One they call Catherine Weldon gave me this pretty thing." He showed Yellow Bird a small gold charm in the shape of a buffalo bull that hung from his watch chain.

"It is the only one the white men have left us, Grandfather."

"Yes, perhaps the only one."

"But, Grandfather, the buffalo will return."

"I have heard that you led Big Foot's people in the ghost dance."

"Yes. The Messiah will come soon, for there are signs everywhere."

"Have you seen the one from the Land of the Grandmother who calls herself Scarlet Woman? She says she will give birth to the new red Jesus."

"You do not believe her, Grandfather?"

"No, nor do you."

"Grandfather, the shaman Kicking Bear has seen Wovoka. Do you not believe him?"

"I believe that he has traveled to the west and seen a preacher. I believe that he believes he climbed a ladder up through the clouds and saw the world to come. The agent McLaughlin has argued with me as you do, Yellow Bird, and I have told him, 'Let us go west together and see this man Wovoka, and then I will return and tell my people whether he is a lie or not.' But McLaughlin will not go. He will not let me go. I have danced. When my daughter died of spotted fever, I danced. I looked for a trance."

"Yes?"

"It did not happen. I have my own visions. Things are painted." He looked toward the gray sky, empty of clouds, without expression. "Perhaps it is the end of the People."

"It is the beginning, Grandfather."

"I have seen a spark coming toward me," said Sitting Bull, "and I have received letters from Mrs. Weldon saying that I am to be murdered. I do not think the whites will do this. Great men are destroyed by those who envy them, and no white envies an Indian."

"No Indian would strike at Sitting Bull."

"You may not, but I rode out one day, and in the treetops a meadow lark sang, 'The Sioux will kill you.' "

"No, Grandfather. They would be afraid to draw their guns."

"I am no longer a warrior."

"There will be a great dance soon at Pine Ridge. Come to it, Grandfather. It will make you see more clearly. You will see your departed ones, your daughter."

"Perhaps. I will take counsel." The old man looked close into Yellow Bird's eyes as if probing for answers there. "Yes, I will go to Pine Ridge."

Yellow Bird left, triumphant. If Sitting Bull danced, all would follow. The Messiah would know then that the People were loyal. The dance would not be trampled out by the agents like a small fire in the grass, as some had tried to do. At Pine Ridge, Daniel Royer, called Young Man Afraid of Indians, had threatened that he would call the bluecoats if they danced. But no one had been hurt by the dancing and the soldiers had not come. Some of the agents relied upon winter to drive the people into their lodges and so put an end to the dancing, but autumn held into the Freezing Moon.

The aging McLaughlin, the agent, was thin, with stiff white hair that made him look like a bedraggled rooster. He rode out in his creaking buggy with his Indian wife, who had been an interpreter with a circus.

"There will be trouble," he said through her. "This is a war dance."

"It is a dance for peace," Yellow Bird replied in English. "We worship your God. What difference does it make how we pray, as long as the prayers are answered?"

"You pray that white men shall die," McLaughlin said, speaking to Yellow Bird directly.

"We pray that they will be gone from our land."

"At Pine Ridge the young braves wear ghost shirts in the dance."

"The Mormons wear white robes, too."

"At Pine Ridge they carry guns."

This Yellow Bird at first denied. "No metal. No guns."

"But at Pine Ridge they do carry guns."

"Then it is because the police went there with guns first."

"Of course," came the agent's reply. "But what matters is that there will be killing. Then the bluecoats will come. Then more killing."

Yellow Bird for an instant wanted to shoot McLaughlin,

but the feeling was quite impersonal. No bullet could truly hurt the white man in the way that Yellow Bird wished to bring pain to that race.

"Young Man Afraid of Indians wishes to have soldiers come," said McLaughlin. "They will come on the train from Omaha. They will be the Seventh Cavalry. They hate your people since the Little Bighorn. The black buffalo soldiers will come, too. It will be very bad for your people if the dancing does not stop."

"It would be worse for my people if it does," Yellow Bird replied.

There was that gulf between them.

"I'm sorry," McLaughlin said. He looked very old then, barely able to flick the reins.

He would help us if he understood, thought Yellow Bird as the old buggy creaked out of sight.

The dancing had to go on. It was more urgent now than ever, and Palmer, the agent at Cheyenne River, could no more stop it there than could McLaughlin at Standing Rock. Then word arrived from Pine Ridge that Short Bull had talked with the Messiah. The Messiah had pledged that, because of the agents' interference, the time for the great change was no longer to be spring, but winter. It would be soon after the time when the white man celebrated the birth of his god. Until then they must dance, even though they were surrounded by soldiers.

That night Yellow Bird dreamed of many buffalo led by a great white bull. As he watched, the bull was attacked. Other bulls fought around him, and when it was over the white bull lay gored among the fallen. "This is a warning," Yellow Bird told himself, "but not for me. It is for Sitting Bull." Should he tell Sitting Bull of the dream? Its portent was as vague as what Sitting Bull had heard himself. Undecided, Yellow Bird visited the Hog Ranch, which stood just outside the Cheyenne River reserve. There red and white men mingled with whiskey and cards and women, and many things were said. The Hog Ranch, which had begun as a migrant whiskey wagon, had become mired one day in the mud and, before its proprietor had sobered up sufficiently to extricate his property, the wheels had rotted. Since then, the remains had been decked over in warped green pine and even expanded, though the roof was still patched canvas. No need for the rag-topped path markers, for from downwind a blind man could have walked straight to the Hog Ranch so strong was the reek of fresh vomit and stale cigars.

Yellow Bird arrived in the quiet afternoon. A mindless tittering told him that Hard to Hit was there as usual. Hard to Hit had served on both sides during the long wars and had dodged successfully every missile that had been flung his way except for a bottle of devil water, which had hit him square between the teeth. He'd clung to its neck ever since and would not let go until he died. Muttering, stupefied, he'd become the innocent double agent who heard and garbled all and passed it on as witlessly as a river passed sewage. He was tipsy now, shambling and staring at shadows. Yellow Bird took him by a wrist and tried to lead him to a bench. Hard to Hit pulled away and fell with a crash of glass. He then refused to move until he was persuaded the wetness on his shirt was rotgut whiskey and not blood. Yellow Bird propped him up and fetched him a fresh bottle, at which he sucked like a baby.

Between swallows, rumors came from his thick tongue, contradictory and overlapping. Buffalo Bill Cody was coming with a wagon full of sweets to take Sitting Bull to jail, his mouth crammed with lollipops. Buffalo Bill was not coming. The Indian agent wished to wait until bad weather when Sitting Bull could not escape. Sitting Bull had said he was going to Pine Ridge, and the army had an arrest order to stop him. Lieutenant Bull Head was already out with his Indian police, and he had sworn to arrest Sitting Bull and kill his mortal enemy, Sitting Bull's chief bodyguard, Catch the Bear. There was no telling which rumor was the latest or which superseded which, but, one way or another, time was running out.

"Hard to Hit, you're a soaker. You'll kill yourself," Yellow Bird told him.

"I'm already dead. I can't hear myself breathe, Yellow Bird, but you'll bring me back with the others?"

"We'll bring you all back," Yellow Bird promised.

There was nothing urgent in Hard to Hit's muddled rumors, but when the white man was involved, there was seldom time to reflect, to smoke a pipe and let a new moon rise. That sense of impatience and urgency which was in Yellow Bird's blood renewed itself with the pound of his pony's hoofs, the struck sparks, the dark swooping shadows of birds. Under his blanket Yellow Bird wore his ghost shirt. He was armed with a bow and with Boggs's pistol. His pony's flanks were painted with jagged lightning for speed, his head with medicine arrows, for no animal so marked had ever been shot. Those were the only precautions he had taken against the dangers ahead, and they seemed good. He did not consider his own life to be in peril and he rode steadily until his pony began to shake its head insistently. "Why do you say no?" he demanded. "You should not be tired." He stopped by a trickle of icy water that ran from the moss-lined bowl of a dead tree. Both drank, then walked side by side as the moon rose. Yellow Bird rode again under a ceiling of high clouds like the broken surface of a thawing lake. Still the pony seemed to say no. Perhaps it was that smell which was no smell, the first dead scent of winter.

Toward dawn, Yellow Bird arrived across the river from Sitting Bull's camp. There, beside the ford, Gray Eagle had his lodge, a black cone against the dawn. As he approached, Yellow Bird noticed men drawn up in a stiff rank. They must be bluecoats, he thought at first. No Indians would stand that way. But they were Indians, or once had been, the uniformed, cropped-haired Indian police, standing side by side at parade rest, their hands folded over the barrels of their rifles. He wished them all in hell, these worse than white men. They were up to no good, he knew that. Feeling sure he would be taken captive if he were seen, Yellow Bird edged up stealthily, keeping to the shadows. He recognized Bull Head, who was taller than the rest and appeared to be in command. He paced the line, pulled a metal time-teller from his pocket, and consulted it. Then there rose Shave Head's voice in derision. "What are you all afraid of? You think the old man will be full of rotgut and gas? You think he will blow us all over dead?" No one denied the possibility, and when Gray Eagle, a convert to the white man's God, stood among them, many knelt to hear him say the Lord's Prayer.

So they were after Sitting Bull already; Yellow Bird guessed that much. He began to work his way around the police until he was between them and the river crossing, but his pony stepped on a twig. A hissed command was flung his way: "Halt or I'll fire!" He did not halt but kicked his pony on, knowing they would not shoot for fear the sound might announce their dark purpose. There was no pursuit. Yellow Bird had scarcely realized this, but when he reined up he saw they had ridden off in the opposite direction. Already they were crossing the misty strip of river. A finger of penetrating light turned the spray to fire. Then the mist, heavy as drizzle, closed overhead. Yellow Bird turned and rode after them. There was no other ford. He was well behind now, but riding fast.

The hooting of owls followed him through the river bottom. "You ride too slow," they seemed to mock. A coyote howled, telling of loneliness and the cold. "Too slow . . . too slow." Up ahead, dogs were barking. When Yellow Bird came within sight of the camp, the police had already arrived. Most lodges were awake and stirring as he galloped through and dismounted just beyond where the police had tethered their horses. He ran on toward Sitting Bull's house where Bull Head, Red Tomahawk, and Shave Head, their pistols drawn, struggled to lean their collective weight against the narrow door. It gave way finally and the cursing trio sprawled inside. By now spectators began to arrive from other lodges. Andrew Fox, Sitting Bull's interpreter, clad in tattered striped trousers, a Prince Albert coat, and a bullet-drilled panama hat, led the way in stately fashion as though he headed a diplomatic mission. Behind him was Catch the Bear. Like many of the younger braves, he was armed, and Yellow Bird had only to glance his way to be sure he was in no mood to parley.

The shouts and screams issuing from the cabin were enough to tell Yellow Bird that Sitting Bull and his women were home. They were being routed unwillingly from bed. Through the door he could dimly see a struggling knot of limbs. The Indian police were trying to dress the old man, as an infant who keeps his arms and legs stiff must be forcibly clad. At the same time they propelled him toward the door, with one leg in his leggings, the other out. "I can dress myself, thank you!" Sitting Bull announced loudly. His was the only calm voice in all that shouting, stumbling confusion. "You need not honor me like this."

More and more spectators were coming up behind Yellow Bird and Andrew Fox, who has his back turned to the cabin now, his arms raised for peace and order. The braves shook saddle bells. Others brandished their rifles and shouted him down, while the chief's two wives, expelled stark naked from their cabin, huddled by the wall chanting, "Sitting Bull, you have always led us. What will happen now?" This seemed to hold Sitting Bull back. At the door he spread-eagled himself against the frame. "You must bring my horse," he commanded. Red Bear and White Bird, both police, went for the old circus horse, Roland, throwing a saddle upon him as they led him back. All the while the crowd grew. Yellow Bird could not count them all as Sitting Bull finally emerged, limping and leaning to one side. Then gradually, as he advanced, he became transformed. He straightened up, seeming younger, more purposeful.

His son, Crow Foot with the twisted foot, called on him to resist. His wives, blanket-wrapped now, howled their death song. Sitting Bull stopped in his tracks, and Red Tomahawk and Lieutenant Bull Head thrust their guns against his back to make him move toward his horse. At that moment Catch the Bear, standing in the path of all three, snapped a cartridge into the chamber of his carbine. Andrew Fox thrust his old panama hat over the muzzle as though that might make the

[193]

gun and the threat, even Catch the Bear, disappear altogether.

Sitting Bull must have seen and weighed it all, for suddenly he shouted, "My people, I will not go!"

The blare of a bugle could have been no more emphatic as a call to arms. Instantly Catch the Bear discharged his leveled gun, drilling another hole through the panama hat. Bull Head opened his mouth and began to crumple, his left hand groping for a well in his thigh that pumped red blood. As he went down, he fired the pistol that he still held against Sitting Bull's side. In the same instant, Red Tomahawk fired point-blank at Sitting Bull, and the veteran of endless battles fell, roaring, the fanged hatred of a rattlesnake in his eyes. Enraged he lay there, and enraged he died.

With Sitting Bull down, things moved faster than Yellow Bird could see or remember. Shave Head crumpled up, clutching his belly. Catch the Bear, his gun misfiring, was clubbed to the ground and shot as he tried to rise. Around the fallen the fight raged in bitter flurries of hatred as relative murdered relative. Crow Foot, trying to limp away, was shot to bits. Braves whom Yellow Bird could not name died on either side. Then, with the clamor of an audience all around him, the old circus horse sat back on his haunches beside his felled master and raised his right fore hoof in what seemed a farewell salute. With the wonder of it, all firing briefly stopped as though only a horse had the respect to mark the passing of a great man. In the respite the surviving police dragged Bull Head's riddled body back to the cabin, which would be their final fortress. For a time bullets hammered against the log walls. Then the bluecoats arrived with their Hotchkiss gun and the Indians withdrew, allowing the confused soldiers time to fire two shells at their allies in the cabin before Red Tomahawk came out with a white flag. The siege was over.

Yellow Bird had withdrawn and watched from the slope. From there he saw the sorting of the dead, the vengeance taken by Holy Medicine whose brother lay dead among the police. This death Holy Medicine must have blamed upon Sitting Bull, who had not fired a shot, for he beat upon the motionless face and body of the chief until his rifle butt broke at the wrist. No Indian dared respond to this indignity, none dared face the big-mouthed guns except Yellow Bird. His blanket cast aside, he rode back and forth, inviting the massed fire of the enemy. A dozen shots cracked out; two dozen. A soldier laughed. They began to cheer his bravery and sheath their guns. Then an officer walked out purposefully, rested his carbine on the stump of a tree, aimed, and fired. Yellow Bird felt the bullet whistle past him. The officer aimed again. This time the gun misfired. The officer tried again and again, then finally threw down his weapon in disgust and walked away. Yellow Bird made one final tour of the hill, his grin fixed and triumphant.

At last he rode off to spread the alarm, for presently soldiers would be after them all: the Seventh Cavalry, who hated all Sioux, and the Ninth, the black buffalo soldiers in their muskrat caps and buffalo-skin overcoats. Only later would he hear how Sitting Bull's body, the face pounded beyond recognition so that some would deny it was he, was thrown into a wagon for the ride to Standing Rock. There it was buried in a bloody blanket under five gallons of chloride of lime and muriatic acid. The great man was laid away like a felon while his people fled from the agency camps into the Badlands to make a feast in honor of their coming Messiah.

IX

Big Foot and the Seventh Cavalry

Yellow Bird was not the only one to carry the news of Sitting Bull's murder. The shock wave spread in every direction. Wherever the story was told, there followed lamentation and fear. Yellow Bird was less disturbed than many that he talked to, for he was confident that Sitting Bull would soon return in triumph, riding at Crazy Horse's side. By the time he reached Big Foot's camp near Cherry Creek, he was living in the future, not the past. Numbers of Hunkpapa had fled ahead of him to the Miniconjou camp, and the chief's lodge was under guard by his warrior society.

The chief was ill. His massive strength was gone. His lips caved in over stubbled teeth and his watery eyes sat large upon his cheekbones. In them was the bewildered look of an old bull that has lost its horns in combat and is called again to battle. Now Big Foot appealed to the young man as one older and stronger than himself.

"What do you advise, Yellow Bird? Am I to flee, as some have done? Or surrender to the pony soldiers?"

"What great chief has surrendered and lived long?" Yellow Bird asked. Receiving no reply from the old chief, he went on. "Hump is a great chief. He has fled to the Badlands. But what of Big Foot? What will he do?" Pride glowed in the sunken eyes for an instant, but then it gave way to the former look of pain and bewilderment. Sickness draws contempt.

"Big Foot is too tired to fight."

Yellow Bird drew his knife and dug it into a knot in one of the lodgepoles as if to affirm his own words. "But Big Foot can flee. He can keep the ghost dance. The pony soldiers would stop the dance, and without the dance the Messiah will not come."

"My people are hungry. I am too sick to mount a pony."

"Then you will die of the coughing sickness. You are sick beyond my medicine. Only the Messiah can save you. Only he will feed your people."

Big Foot looked for strength inside himself and saw only pain. "If the ghost shirt would stop the coughing . . ."

"Better to die quickly as brave men obeying the commands of the Great Spirit than to die slowly, as cowards at the agency door."

"I hear you, Yellow Bird. You are right, but there are few warriors, and it is hard."

"Grandfather, when the time comes, there will be warriors without end."

The old chief nodded. "You may tell the people to strike their lodges," he said.

So the Miniconjou people went into the Badlands with a north wind behind them. It brought clouds, but no snow. There was still dry grass for the ponies, and a few cattle that had strayed from the ranches. Within two days the cattle were eaten, but hunger and the howling of wolves stayed with the People. In the faces of the women and children was the worn beauty of the prairie itself, the tale of their dwindling race. Their features were pictographs of battles, defeats, retreats, migrations. There was no song left in the women, no play in the children, who sat in the sun seeking warmth that was not there. Though in Yellow Bird's mind their suffering could not last long, the children roused him to prayer. "O my Father, pity these children. All their food is gone." The response was almost immediate. An overturned wagon was found, full of a cargo of salt pork and bacon. It was so spoiled it had been ignored by the wolves, but the people devoured it. The meat was slippery as wet soap, and many were sick. Some began then to disappear, heading on their own to the agencies. Others departed when word spread of chiefs—No Flesh, Two Strikes, and even Hump—who had made their peace with the bluecoats. Hump, the great warrior, was now out scouting for the army.

"Then he is a shavehead," Yellow Bird said to Big Foot. "You are the only real Indian chief left."

"But Hump is alive," Big Foot replied.

"In a few days he will vanish with his white friends," Yellow Bird informed him. The time was so close. That night he climbed the nearest hill and scanned the black horizon for hostile fires. The People had lived so long on the reservation that most had lost their gift for hiding a trail. Others no longer cared. The night was black and silent; if it had secrets, it kept them. Before dawn, Yellow Bird awoke with the rolling report of attack in his ears. "Big-mouthed guns," he said aloud, but it was only ice breaking up in the river. "Give me this day. Give me this last week," he prayed.

Two days before the one upon which the white men celebrated the first coming of the Messiah, bluecoats were reported moving toward them from the north. The Indians began trekking south toward Red Cloud's agency at Pine Ridge. On Christmas Day they passed a white ranch and heard voices raised in songs of praise. By now Big Foot had given up any attempt to ride and lay jolting in his wagon like an old and stricken owl, all claw and beak and bedraggled feathers, his arms as limp as broken wings. He breathed in gurgles and snorts, and his fits of coughing hawked up living tissue. Yet somehow his dignity held, as well as his command, and he kept the braves from ravaging the ranch for food.

Christmas had passed when the first army scout, Little Bat, caught up with them. They were moving more slowly now toward Porcupine Creek. It took the scout only one day to ride off with his report and another for the army to appear. The first warning was a group of outriders, who galloped in, waving their blankets. Then from the horizon came a column of black dots, moving slowly, terribly, across the waste. Some families fled, seeking gullies and caves to hide in. By midday the pony soldiers had come close enough for Yellow Bird to recognize the red and blue swallowtail guidon of the Seventh Cavalry. Four troops moved up, two on either side. The Indians kept on doggedly, ready to fight and die, until Big Foot croaked out his last command and had a white flag run up from his wagon.

They were flanked completely by troopers now, and Yellow Bird deployed the braves. Slowly the hostile columns converged, the soldiers in their bulky buffalo coats looking as though they fed on great haunches of red meat, the braves in their rags of agency cloth and ancient rawhide as if they lived on lizards and grasshoppers. The explosion might have come at any moment and yet the friction never drew the incendiary spark. The memory of bugles and faded flags seemed to dim.

A Major Whiteside rode up. He was in temporary command. Big Foot staggered to his feet. Though his nose dripped blood, he managed to say, "We want only peace. My people . . ."

The major cut him off summarily. "I'm not bargaining. Surrender or fight."

The old chief swayed forward and back. The frost at his feet was speckled with crimson. "Surrender," he whispered.

The major nodded, turned to an aide, commanded an ambulance to be brought forward. Big Foot did not resist. He needed help to board. Again all moved forward as before. The Indians, still carrying their weapons, were sandwiched between the flanking troopers on the long road from the battle on the Greasy Grass that led toward Pine Ridge. On the way was Wounded Knee Creek, where Crazy Horse and Worm still lay. Memory stirred in Yellow Bird. After all these years of flight and war, so few remained alive from his childhood that the emptiness was peopled with ghosts. Before them all stood Crazy Horse, riding back now through endless skies of remembrance, larger than life.

Yellow Bird tried to visit Big Foot, but the soldiers put him aside, saying that the chief slept in the ambulance. He did not sleep. Yellow Bird heard his breath sliding in his chest like a knife in a sandy sheath. He saw the old chief's eyes, burned out, blank, relying on the army doctors to ease his pain in this life rather than upon Yellow Bird to give him peace in the next. Very well. Perhaps it was meant to be this way from the beginning. It was to be his task alone.

Behind them, the sunset glowed through ragged clouds as they descended from high ground toward Wounded Knee Creek. Beside its bank did Crazy Horse lie and listen, impatient now at the sound of hoofs, eager to burst from the frost-sparkled soil and announce the new day? "Soon," Yellow Bird told him. "It will be soon now."

The sun lay briefly on the horizon, its rays as cheerless as a burned-out star. Then night fell. It was too late for the soldiers to try to disarm them, but they surrounded the camp with its one hundred and twenty braves of fighting age or older, and twice that number of women and children. Yellow Bird watched as a stove was brought to Big Foot's tent. "Major Whiteside tries to win him that way," he thought. The bluecoat chiefs set up their lodges near Louis Mosseau's trading post. During the night, more bluecoats arrived. The rumor spread that Whiteside had been replaced by Colonel Forsyth, commander of the Seventh Cavalry, of which Custer had been commander years ago. With him had come four big-mouthed guns and more troopers, men, it was said, who had been with Reno and Benteen at the Greasy Grass. They looked tired and cold in the firelight and, when they tried stacking their arms, the guns kept falling with a brittle clatter, like icicles breaking off. They had three times the Indians' fighters, Yellow Bird reckoned, but it wasn't numbers that counted now.

After the soldiers had eaten, a huge black pot of stew was carried to the Indian children, who waited solemnly for the signal to begin. Only when the soldiers left did they attack the still-steaming pot with stolid ferocity.

When both camps were quiet, Yellow Bird called a council of the braves. Big Foot was too sick to attend. In his fever and delirium, he had already gone before to that world which Yellow Bird so eagerly awaited. All who came were exhausted and despairing. They had long since eaten what remained of their provisions, and they were gripped by a torpor born of unsatiated hunger. It could not numb their gloom, nor did it muffle the steady trudge of boots on frozen ground. Yellow Bird spoke first. "We must declare war," he said, an expression of the white man's that for him had dignity and a feeling of equality in arms. "We have no reason to be afraid. It is the soldiers who must fear us. They know we are protected by the ghost shirts, and that soon the Messiah whom they hung up with nails will come as an angry flame. Then their horses and their big-mouthed guns will sink into the earth and they will all follow."

Some embraced his words; others were possessed by angry doubts. White Bull shouted back, "Yellow Bird, your eyes are full of smoke, your ears full of thunder. Braves, this talk is for children. You will die like rabbits hunted down by wolves in the snow."

"We speak of different worlds," Yellow Bird asserted. "Yours is dying. The sacred tree falls. The hoop is broken. You must choose. This will be the last war. The Great Spirit would not make so many preparations if he did not plan to build the future of our people on this fight."

Much talk went back and forth. Were the ghost shirts invulnerable? Would the soldiers really fall down as if the bones had dissolved in their flesh? "We will not see them die that easily," White Bull insisted. "They have the iron horse, the big-mouthed guns, the singing wire. They are too clever."

"It may be a hard fight," Yellow Bird conceded, "but we have wisdom in council, courage in battle, and belief in the Messiah. We will win. But even if we were to die, better that it be fighting than watching our children die of starvation."

No one opinion prevailed, and in the end it was decided to turn over only a token of broken guns to the soldiers. The best ones would be hidden. A fight was to be avoided if possible, but if that fight were to come, few wished to rely on faith alone. So Yellow Bird let it stand. The night was almost over. Presently it would not matter, and it seemed meaningless that beneath his new ghost shirt, rainbow-painted, streaked with red lightning, was the cold weight of Bill Boggs's loaded pistol. He relied on more powerful weapons now, more powerful allies than the exhausted braves around him. There was Crazy Horse buried nearby. His blood called to Yellow Bird. It sang of that victory which would change the world. Yellow Bird's faith by now had lost its exuberance. It had turned to ice, but it was as fixed as the polar star.

While the others curled up and slept, Yellow Bird prayed: "Grandfather, behold my people. Guide them. The fires have grown cold. The old songs are forgotten. Hear my prayer and lead your children to safety. All things belong to you: the hills, the sky, the four-leggeds and the two-leggeds. You have said I must send a cry, once to each quarter of the earth, and now I call. Help us. Make your people wait no longer. You have spoken to me from the thunder. You have shown me the white buffalo. Now make the sacred hoop whole again." His vision blurred. He seemed to see a rainbow before him. "Great Spirit, the sacred tree is withered. Make it bloom. Make it bloom while some of your people are still alive."

The wind was fitful, flung from a starless sky. It cut his lungs like a damp blade. Snow should come. With the first tinge of milkiness in the air, Yellow Bird heard one, then several army mules announcing in seesawing lament the coming day. A bugle stitched out a brisk refrain. Time, whether measured by the white man's metal heart or by the moon and the sun, was running out.

There was no sun that morning. The sky was an iron sheet. A storm was building. Yellow Bird could smell the snow that would come. The high and singing wind was from the north, a wind driven by that other storm he had so long awaited. He could hear them riding behind the clouds, allies no big-mouthed gun could fell. Four of those wagon guns stared down now from the rise of ground across the camp, dumb and open-mouthed. He'd seen the soldiers fire them once at a herd of antelope. One crashing flash, and in the wreathing smoke the herd lay torn and floundering. They would not kill today.

The mingled smell of bacon and coffee came from the soldiers' fires. The surgeon entered Big Foot's tent and came out again. When Yellow Bird visited his chief, the old man did not seem to recognize him. "What did they give him?" he demanded of the women there, and they looked afraid and could not say. He would have prayed for the chief, that he might have strength for one more day, but he heard the crier outside announcing that the braves were to assemble for a talk with the soldier chief before moving on to the Pine Ridge reservation. Big Foot was lifted from his tent and placed where the older men could gather around him. All the men were packed close together. Then dismounted troopers of the Seventh Cavalry surrounded them, forming a hollow square. Yellow Bird glanced about at that wall of blue and felt like game in a trap.

"You must surrender your guns," an interpreter announced. Yellow Bird had been expecting that. Two ancient trade guns were presented. The interpreter consulted with the soldier chief. "They are not enough. If you will not give us the guns, your camp will be searched." Big Foot looked oblivious of what was happening. Yellow Bird and the other men were silent. The interpreter turned, shook his head. A search party was already pushing toward the tepees occupied now only by the women and children. Bedding was torn apart, parfleches emptied onto the ground, the clothing of the women roughly examined, while the braves, under gunpoint, sat grimly listening to the screams of their families. Big Foot tried weakly to rise and speak. Perhaps he meant to restrain his warriors. He struggled only to his knees, as though in prayer.

"Behold!" Yellow Bird shouted. "He prays to the Messiah. The bluecoats cannot harm you."

The searchers made piles of what they had found. Axes, awls, tent stakes, a few rusty, mostly broken guns lay amid the strewn bedding and scattered clothing. "That is not all. You had more guns yesterday," the interpreter insisted. He barked out his words, and the cold punctuated each one with a white cloud. What he said was true. The good guns, the few they had, were under the blankets of the braves, beneath ghost shirts that hid them and kept them warm, so that hands would not freeze to icy barrels.

A signal brought the ring of soldiers closer, to within ten yards of the seated braves. Only Yellow Bird rose to his feet, and the sight of the vast plain stretching away to dark hills lifted his spirits and extinguished his last doubts. Long after, they would surely sing of this day, as he began singing now. "Take heart. The bullets will not touch you. Take heart . . ." and he dragged his left foot, slowly dancing for the last time.

"Stop that fool medicine man!" He scarcely heard the command, for what he hearkened to was above the braves, beyond the ring of guns, above the prairies his people had once owned, beyond the mountaintops, in the rolling clouds. At last they were coming. Their horses' manes were flowing, the feathers of their war bonnets were streaming back. They were charging at last through seas of prairie grass: Crazy Horse, Black Kettle, the warriors of legends, and with them rose the thunderous rumble of the buffalo. "Now," he chanted, "they come.

Look, you can see them!" He raised his arm to the boiling, glowing clouds.

"Get that man!"

Two soldiers strode toward Yellow Bird. They mattered not. He was transfigured in his strength, a newly forged weapon. Before they could touch him, he raised his eagle-bone whistle to blow them out of existence. Then, without warning, a brave, Black Coyote, rose between them. His eyes were wide. He had been deaf from birth, but he responded to voices the others did not hear. He believed, and he pulled his carbine from under his blanket. A soldier grabbed for it. He spun the brave halfway around and the gun discharged into the air. An instant of silence passed, long enough for the human heart to fill and empty itself. Then there was the roar of guns.

The troopers fired point-blank. As most of the braves were still seated, many of the bullets traveled high, cutting down the bluecoats beyond. His ghost shirt had protected Yellow Bird from the first volley. Others, fashioned with deficient magic, blossomed with blood, but those braves who had not been struck threw their blankets aside and drew out their carbines, repeaters against the soldiers' single-loaders. At less than ten yards, the massacre was terrible. Others, without firearms, lunged at the bluecoats with knives and clubs. Then, from the hill, the big-mouthed guns began to fire in quick succession. First came the coughing thud of discharge; then the air was filled with the whistle and scream of flung metal.

More soldiers appeared, while among the tepees furious white flowers of smoke bloomed and dropped in murky streamers. Yellow Bird aimed his pistol into the smoke where blue figures staggered. An officer lunged at him with his revolver aimed. Both fired at once. When the smoke cleared the man was down, his mouth open and sucking for air like a beached fish. Knees, hands, all were compressed around his stomach where the bullet had entered. Yellow Bird knelt beside him, astonished by the bloody destruction one shot had made. Then something hot as a branding iron touched his wrist. He'd been hit; only a grazing memento, and not where the ghost shirt protected him. But the very fact seemed a warning of mortality, and he drew back in confusion. Retreating, he stumbled over Big Foot, whose riddled body had sprawled backward, his prayerful knees buckled under him.

The sucking black pull of an explosive shell hurled Yellow Bird face down into the chief's tent. He lay there with a roaring in his skull. It was the sound of warriors riding down the sullen clouds, passing overhead. "Hear them!" he shouted, rallying the braves. "Hear them!" he shrieked at the soldiers as they advanced through the acrid smoke with their own cry of "Remember the Little Bighorn!" In his blast-blackened hand Yellow Bird still held his pistol, and he emptied it into their righteous faces.

Then something struck him. At first it seemed only like an injection of firewater directly into his bloodstream. He could not admit the possibility that the ghost shirt had failed. Finally raising his left arm, he saw the hole welling darkly. He could lift his arm no longer but let it drop, keeping it close against his ribs while he went on loading and firing. There was a flaming inside him now, and he was down without being aware of having fallen. Bullets pricked holes in the canvas above his head as he lay there, seeing from bloodshot eyes the brief flurry of that last fight at Wounded Knee. When the lodge caught fire, he began to squirm away. "Crazy Horse," he whispered, "Crazy Horse, help me."

Big Foot and the Seventh Cavalry

Part of him walked through the Black Hills in springtime, smiled at familiar faces, heard the song of birds. Another part stirred and groaned, felt something cold on face and hands. A voice only partly his own said, "I'm cold. There is snow in my blanket. I hurt. I hurt inside." The green hills were veiled in mist, lost altogether. There hung about him the hush of the seventh day of creation. Then came a human voice and a round outline against the sky. "My poor soul," it said. He was being lifted, roughly this time. He was a larva sewn into a dark cocoon of agony.

From bright and biting cold he was moved to a place of dampness and dark, like the cave full of paintings where he had sheltered as a boy. He was wrapped in blankets now. It was only with an effort that he could draw up his legs, then straighten them as the pain returned. There was something large and wet inside him as though he had swallowed a steaming rag. His eyes adjusted to the gloom and he seemed to see Crazy Horse towering above him, his arms outthrust, his hand fixed to a wooden cross. "Can you hear me?" Crazy Horse seemed to say. He nodded in reply. "Do you say prayers?" Again he nodded and then the prayers began in a voice he did not recognize. "The Lord is my shepherd. . . . He maketh me to lie down in green pastures."

"God," he said aloud, and then, "Crazy Horse," and "God" again softly, while the other voice murmured, "Jesus, in thee I die, Jesus . . ." It was the whisper of spring streams gurgling over mossy rocks. "I am the resurrection and the life, saith the Lord: he that believeth in me, though he were dead, yet shall he live. . . ." The voice and the stream droned on together. The dark hovering shape from which it issued faded, became iridescent: Crazy Horse in his loincloth, his hands curled like shells around the nailheads and all of it folding and unfolding as though seen through warped glass. Only then did Yellow Bird notice it. Not as large as he had imagined in visions, but green and living and real, covered with glistening fruit. The promise was fulfilled before his eyes. He had been dying once in a dream, but now he roused himself and cried out, "The sacred tree lives. It lives!" Then Crazy Horse seized him gently and bore him up. Light faded, and he was lost in the blackness of thrashing wings.

X

Walking the Black Road

No gods or ghost shirts had shielded them at Wounded Knee. They had fought as brave men with no more than human skill and so they had died. For two days and nights after the battle, the snow moaned, and it was not the wind's voice but that of the wounded. Most of the dead and injured were women and children, blasted apart by the Hotchkiss guns. Those who ran from the explosions to hide in gullies were hunted down by troopers and butchered. Two miles from the battlefield they were cut down and left to freeze, and they were covered by the snow in attitudes of fear and helpless self-defense. Big Foot, the first to fall, lay back, his eyes oddly twinkling with frost, a bizarre mask mocking the living with one arm raised, the fingers beckoning.

On January 1, 1891, a pit was opened and the dead were shoveled into it. Many were naked, since the ghost shirts were in demand as souvenirs. When missionaries came to read over the common grave, Colonel Forsyth turned them away, saying, "Let the red devils go to hell without a prayer." So the earth was poured back over the uncounted dead, perhaps one hundred and fifty men, women, and children, perhaps more, with only wooden posts to mark the place. Later these posts were smeared with sacred red paint. That was all. At Wounded Knee, the Indian wars came to an end. Fifty years before, the

Indian had owned the West. Now indeed the superintendent of the United States Census could record without fear of contradiction that the frontier had ceased to exist.

Not all were dead upon the field or buried under it. A few survived wounds and the blizzard that followed. A baby girl of three months was found under the snow, carefully wrapped in a blanket, beside her dead mother. On her head was a buckskin cap decorated with a beaded American flag. Later she was adopted by the commander of the Nebraska state troops. She would be baptized Marguerite. Her Indian name remained Zilkala-noni, meaning Lost Bird.

Those wounded who were picked up after the fight were loaded into open wagons and taken to Pine Ridge, where they lay throughout the bitter night while prospects for shelter were laboriously discussed. Toward morning, benches were cleared from the Episcopalian mission. Hay was spread upon the floor and the wounded were brought in to lie under the decorations of evergreen and popcorn and cheesecloth banners proclaiming "Peace on Earth, Good Will to Men." Quickly the church filled with the sounds of suffering and death. Here many died as the decorated Christmas tree glowed in their eyes, filling their delirium with the expectation of hope at last fulfilled.

The business of Wounded Knee did not entirely end with the burying of the dead. General Miles would presently bring charges against Colonel Forsyth for precipitating a massacre. The charges would be summarily dismissed. Instead, Forsyth would receive a commendation from the War Department, and eighteen of his Seventh Cavalry troopers would receive the Congressional Medal of Honor.

Nor was the Messiah instantly forgotten. In December of 1890 a white man named Albert Hopkins, wrapped in a blanket and claiming to be the Indian Messiah, had appeared at Pine Ridge. His intention was to carry the "Pansy Banner of Peace" into the Badlands, but Red Cloud would have none of him and Hopkins was ejected from the reservation. Undaunted, he wrote to the Secretary for Indian Affairs three years later: "With the help of the Pansy and its motto and manifest teaching, 'Union, Culture and Peace,' and the star-pansy banner, of which I enclose an illustration, I hope to establish the permanent peace of the border." He signed it "Albert C. Hopkins, Pres. Pro. Tem., The Pansy Society of America." His request was denied, and he wrote again, this time as the Indian Messiah, indicating that he would and must go before the prairie pansies bloomed. He was not heard from again.

The Indians' own hope for a Messiah died more slowly. The ghost dance, forbidden along with the sun dance, was practiced in secret, but it gradually fell into disuse. The older sun dance was revived at carnivals and rodeos, but never as Sitting Bull had performed it at the Greasy Grass. His sacred pole would stand abandoned for years, rot finally to a stump, then vanish entirely. Not long after, in a hut on the shores of Lake Walker, Wovoka died, on October 4, 1932, the impoverished prophet of a forgotten Messiah.

Even so, the battle of Wounded Knee was to be revived. Four times a bill was introduced in Congress to compensate the survivors, only to be forgotten in the late 1930's when a greater crime war was brewing. It is hard to bring back dead days. Only the objects that clustered around the events can be preserved. Briefly, in 1972, the two came together. An Indian, Yellow Thunder, had been killed. A crowd gathered in protest, the most impassioned going by bus and car down the Pine Ridge reservation road known as the Big Foot Trail to the museum and trading post that stand near Wounded Knee. There Clive Gildersleeve had put together an irreplaceable collection of Sioux relics. Shouting, "Burn, burn, burn," the crowd, mostly teen-agers who would once have been called braves, stormed through the trading post, tore posters picturing General Custer from the walls, and knocked over a popcorn stand entitled "Custer's Last Stand." Then they raced on to the museum, destroying or looting most of its treasures, a sad echo of a gallant rage.

Less than a year later Wounded Knee was once again a battleground, when two hundred Oglala Sioux, led by militants of the American Indian Movement, set up barricades there and pledged to die rather than surrender to the surrounding troops and federal marshals. At the heart of this seventy-day stand were a new Indian pride and self-awareness, the wish to take charge of their own affairs, and a desire for civil rights that promises to intensify.

However successful the Indians are in their struggle, there is no way to bring back the old days. It can only be hoped that a new day is dawning for them. At least Yellow Bird's vision of Crazy Horse as a giant riding in the clouds is now more fact than fancy. On Thunderhead Mountain, a statue is being carved out. Financed by the Crazy Horse Memorial Commission, the job is being done with dynamite, air compressor drills, and bulldozers. It will require the moving of eighteen million tons of rock. When complete, the length of Crazy Horse's arm alone will be more than that of a football field. The arm is important, for the sculpture of the chief on a rearing war pony was inspired by a story. When a white man asked Crazy Horse where his land was, the chief stretched out his arm, pointing ahead, and said, "My land is where my people lie buried." It is to be hoped that this statement can be modified in time, and a Sioux chief will be able to say with pride, "My land is where my people live."

Historical Note

The Indians and whites who appear in this book are primarily real people, and the events in which they take part actually happened. An Indian princess, captured after the Battle of the Washita, did become the mother of General Custer's son. The boy was called Yellow Bird. Years later, an Indian medicine man who believed devoutly in the ghost dance religion was present with Chief Big Foot at Wounded Knee, and was in part responsible for provoking that massacre. His name was Yellow Bird. Whether the two Yellow Birds are one and the same is in doubt. Some opinion suggests that General Custer's son died as a boy. In any event, there is no accurate record of his life from 1876 at the Little Bighorn until 1890 and Wounded Knee, but the retreat from the Little Bighorn, the pursuit of the Indian bands in the Big Horns and in the Black Hills, the killing of Crazy Horse, and the flight to Canada all took place as described.

Later, many Indians did go to New York and England with Wild West shows, and European royalty did ride in the performing coach acts there. But there is no indication that a Yellow Bird was among the Indian performers or that any of the guns were loaded with live ammunition. Deer Walking is a fiction, though Bill Boggs was in fact a small-time cattle rustler and died in a gunfight with the law. Only his *BB*-marked pistol survives.

At this point, the ghost dance faith had begun its spread eastward from Wovoka's home in Nevada, and it was encouraged among the Sioux by the medicine men mentioned here. Among them was Yellow Bird, whose faith in a dream placed Big Foot and his people on the trail that led to death at the creek called Wounded Knee.